the
FLYING CLOUD
clipper
1851
1874

Every hour that I was not in school, found me down at the wharves watching the loading and the unloading, listening to the talk of sailormen and the rousing chanteys.

All Sail Set
A romance of the Flying Cloud

written and illustrated by
ARMSTRONG SPERRY

introduction by William McFee

David R. Godine, Publisher, Inc.
BOSTON

This is a Nonpareil Book
first published in 1984 by
DAVID R. GODINE, PUBLISHER, INC.
Box 450
Jaffrey, New Hampshire 03452
website: www.godine.com

Library of Congress Cataloging in Publication Data
Sperry, Armstrong, 1897–
All sail set.
Title on added t.p.: The Flying Cloud,
clipper, 1851–1874
Reprint. Originally published: Chicago: Winston, 1935.
Summary: When his father loses his fortune, a boy is
taken on by a famous shipbuilder and eventually makes
a maiden, record-breaking trip around Cape Horn
on the "Flying Cloud."
1. McKay, Donald, 1810–1880–Juvenile fiction.
2. Flying Cloud (ship)–Juvenile fiction. [1. McKay,
Donald, 1810-1880–Fiction. 2. Flying Cloud (Ship)–
Fiction. 3. Clipper ships–Fiction. 4. Sea stories]
I. Title. II. Title Flying Cloud, clipper, 1851-1874
PZ7.S49A   1984   [Fic]   84-47650
ISBN 0-87923-523-3

Fifth printing, 2003

Printed in the United States of America

This book about a ship
is inscribed to the
memory of

CAPTAIN SERENO ARMSTRONG

by his great-grandson

INTRODUCTION

IT MIGHT be supposed, with sailing ships becoming more and more of a curiosity every year, and with so many excellent books on the subject following one another from the press, that little remains to be told of the famous days of sail. On the contrary, from certain signs of the times, it appears that sea literature is entering upon a new lease of life, and many tales have yet to be published, neither romantic nor sensational, but genuinely truthful and realistic narratives of the lives of deep-water mariners.

The maritime history of New England in the first part of the nineteenth century has certain features not found elsewhere in the world. A stormy, difficult coast; a hardy race of men, who were also born traders; an almost unlimited supply of oak and pine suitable for shipbuilding, and a network of manufacturing centers—all these combined to produce a shipping community second to none. It is not enough to have ships coming into harbor and merchants with cargoes to consign. True maritime prosperity arises when men take naturally, without immediate thought of money

making, to ships and shipbuilding, when whole families are so saturated with seafaring thoughts that it becomes the natural way of life for boys to adopt, and the girls accept as part of their existence the absence of their husbands and sweethearts for long voyages.

It was only natural, moreover, that the development of faster and larger vessels should take place along the shores of New England and Canada. This was the most densely settled section of the American continent, and the demand for tonnage was keener here than elsewhere. The discoveries of Bowditch and Maury made possible a speed unknown before. It was not seriously believed that the new-fangled steamboats which Samuel Cunard was building would ever compete with sails in transporting cargoes. The cost of fuel was too great. A new design of windship was coming into vogue to maintain the prestige of New England, vessels with long, knifelike bows and a vast spread of canvas, built on the lines of a fish so that speed could be maintained in light winds. The clipper ship was the deep-water man's answer to the challenge of the steamboat, and when gold was discovered in California, the opportunity came to show the world what he could do. The greatest naval architect of the day was given practically *carte blanche* by shipowners to design the fastest and finest ship possible. Donald McKay produced many magnificent vessels, but his shipyard never gave birth and being to anything that captured the imaginations and the hearts of men so completely as did his *Flying Cloud*.

Flying Cloud had a long career for a ship of her class. The tremendous spread of canvas and the relentless driving by their captains in search of a record, strained all the clippers so much that they were soon used up. They were, as shipwrights say, unduly spent. Compare the few short years of such ships with *Erin's Isle*, built in 1877 in my father's yard at Saint John, N. B., about the same tonnage and rig as *Flying Cloud*, but not designed for speed. She sailed the seas for nearly forty years and then became a coal hulk, not because she was worn out, but for lack of charters. The driving of the clipper ships was the last desperate attempt of sail to compete with steam. There was something heroic about that challenge. But as H. M. Tomlinson says somewhere, rather grimly, ships make time but steamers keep it. There was, in the long run, no possible chance for the windship. She went down gloriously, a thing of beauty that had outlived her day.

Flying Cloud is the heroine of this story of a boy's start at sea. Enoch Thacher, who tells the story in his old age, is the son of a worthy merchant who had lost his fortune when *Empress of Asia* went down with all hands off Cape Horn. To help his mother, Enoch goes to Donald McKay, who knew his father, and takes a position in the drafting room in McKay's yard while *Flying Cloud* is on the stocks. His love for ships and the sea has been fostered by his old friend, Messina Clarke, a shellback of the old-school, who looked with distrust upon McKay's long, concave clipper bows, even when the ships made record passages. Enoch becomes a devoted worshiper of McKay, and the dream of his life is to go to sea. At fifteen his vocation is plain before him. He has learned every rope and spar in the shipyard. He has seen *Flying Cloud* go out in ballast to load in New

York for San Francisco and China. To his joy, Donald McKay recommends him for a cadetship and wins over his widowed mother to consent. Enoch takes the coach to New York and joins the *Cloud* in South Street.

The pattern of all books that tell of boys going to sea is no doubt *Two Years Before the Mast*. But Richard Henry Dana was a special case. He was a young Harvard man who took a voyage around the Horn a hundred years ago. He was not a sailor in the professional sense any more than are the young collegers who sail as summer cadets in our steamers. This is not to depreciate the achievement of Dana as a seaman or the classic that he wrote on his return. It is merely to point out that ships are not manned by collegers, but by boys and men who have so great a passion for the life that they keep on with it in spite of all the hardships and privations. It is a passion which for good or ill is born in many boys, even though they live far inland and have no immediate contact with the sea. When they grow up in a shipping community, the craving becomes irresistible. The sea calls and will not be denied.

In one sense this story of young Enoch Thacher's voyage around the Horn is not fiction at all. The test of good fiction is that it shall produce the impression of truth and this test Mr. Sperry's story of Enoch Thacher's adventures passes triumphantly. The youngest boy who has learned to read will have his nose in this book until he has finished it or his elders have taken it away from him to read themselves. There is a most wholesome atmosphere of realism and truth in this book. Many sea writers are out, not to tell the truth about seafaring, but to make sensational

disclosures. As one who comes from a seafaring and ship-building family, the legends of sailing ships have always appeared to me heavily loaded with bunkum. The notion that every captain was a hard-boiled autocrat and every first mate a bloodthirsty lunatic has always been a shade too fantastical for one whose relatives since 1840 have been masters and mates in sail and steam. That going to sea was no picnic in the days of the windships is doubtless true, but the life appealed to those who had a bent that way, and mates who crippled and murdered their men were in a minority at all times. They received more publicity than decent officers, and their deeds have always appealed to newspapermen and writers of sea stories as better adapted to sensational tales.

This sort of exaggeration is excellently avoided in Mr. Sperry's dashing tale. Everyone on board, from Captain Josiah Perkins Creesy to the boys in the half deck, is a genuine and authentic character. The action that goes on in the narrative is entirely rational and free from the sensational savagery which has been so popular in so many sea stories. As an example, who does not know the sea yarn in which the trembling, green boy is ordered aloft as soon as he is on board? How often have we read of the bucko mate whose idea of efficiency and skill is to lay out several of his men with quite incomprehensible brutality? Mr. Sperry's story is quite different. It is all the more exciting because words and actions ring true. The autocratic captain is there, but he is a human being. Even the bucko mate is there, but what happens to him must be read in the book. The story is full of carefully concealed ingenuity and

inventiveness. The conversation between the captain and the mate while arguing over the handling of the ship is one of the most convincing pieces of realism I have read during a number of years of reading sea literature. The fight between Enoch Thacher and the sea lawyer, Jeeter Sneed, is first-rate. Jeeter, a common type in sea fiction, and usually so overdrawn as to be incredible, is well done here. The mutiny, one of the most easily bungled scenes in any book of this kind, is the real thing. Any boy who does not revel in the Neptune initiations which take place while *Flying Cloud* is crossing the Equator, must be hard to please.

Those days, of course, are gone, never to return. The boy of today who goes to sea has another tale to tell. He does not have to go aloft to fist canvas in a gale nor does he ever see Cape Stiff in winter. It would be foolish to imagine, however, that he has to be any less courageous or ready-witted. At any moment he may be tested. The sea will never be tamed or civilized. The larger and more complex the vessel the more severe the demands upon the personnel. Behind the most ingenious mechanical inventions there must ever be a man's courage, integrity, and presence of mind. All the fine qualities of the human mind and character which are depicted in this tale of *Flying Cloud's* maiden voyage around the Horn are needed today. Boys with the right stuff in them will take Enoch to their hearts and treasure with pride and affection the memory of that lovely ship.

William McFee

CONTENTS

❀

LIST OF ILLUSTRATIONS

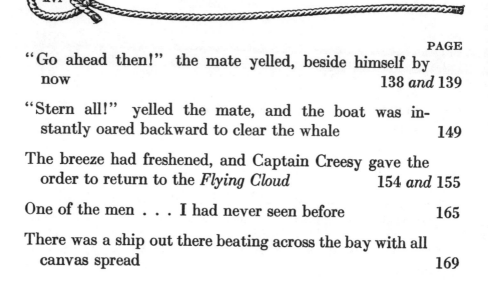

CHAPTER I

I Meet Donald McKay—and Swear a Vow

IF, BY the grace of God, I should live three years longer, I will be one hundred years old. Aye, a ripe age, any way you look at it. There are trees in California—sequoias, they call them—that have seen a thousand winters; there are insects that are born and die before a minute ends. Well— a man's life sails its course between these extremes. Three-score and ten the Bible says. But shucks! That's scarce a babe's age when you're ninety-seven!

Funny thing about age—it's like climbing a mountain. When you're nigh the top, you turn to look back now and again. If your eyesight's good (and mine is as keen as a petrel's, if I do say it as shouldn't) you can pick things out in the valley: men going about their chores; a dog lying in the sun; the river where it turns under the bridge. Memory's like that, too. Just cast your eye back along it when you've most reached the century mark and you'll see a powerful lot of things. Of course they don't all stand out alike. Some are kind of blurry around the edges, and some are so faint you can scarce see them at all. But there are others, plenty of them, clear and sharp.

1

I remember—why, by the Great Horn Spoon! I remember seeing slaves up on the block, being sold at public auction. I remember Lincoln's funeral, and the fever that ran through the country when Booth was captured. I recall, when I was only a shaver of six, squaring off to fight Charles Dickens because he called Americans "savages," and it got my dander up.

Big things were happening. There was a young fellow named Sam Morse who turned his back on a promising career as a portrait painter to tinker with the telegraph. Blatherskite, sober folks called him. Matthew Maury was working out his theory of the natural laws governing winds and currents; charting those "sea lanes," down which the California clippers were to sail to everlasting glory. Steam and the Ericsson screw were turning the maritime world keel up. Steam paddle boats could do eight and nine knots in an hour. The age was crying speed—more speed! If America hoped to compete with the subsidies and monopolies of the Old World, her ships must show their heels to all rivals.

In England Samuel Cunard had established his famous steamship line. When his *Britannia*, snorting like a grampus, pulled into Boston Harbor in the summer of 1840, public enthusiasm swept high. Here was the proper challenge to fan into flame the spark of the American genius for shipbuilding. The windships sharpened their bows, adjusted their sprits to a keener angle, and cracked on more and more sail to hold their own against the invader. The bluff-bowed East Indiamen were doomed; it was sundown for them and dawn for the clipper. Roaring days, those, of iron fists and hearts of oak! America's Golden Age on the sea. But it

was a losing fight. Sometimes I envy the men who, unlike myself, never lived to see the finish: steam's triumph over sail.

The old ships are gone, and the men who manned them. Floating hotels driven by engines have taken their place. Ingenious inventions, I grant you. But ships? Ho! Funny thing about the art of shipbuilding—men practiced it for centuries before they produced the grand clippers of the '50's. But it died almost within a decade. The engine won out. The art has gone, like the ships themselves. And gone are the wildest, sweetest, freest years of life. So, in these latter days, you must pardon an old man while he casts his eye backward and remembers the days when life was as fresh as a morning at sea, and the sky was swept by the winds of surprise.

Show me the boy who doesn't love ships! East Boston, where I was born, was a small lad's paradise, for here ships were built; here they set sail for voyages to the world's end; here they returned, heavy with ivory and pearl shell and oil and whalebone. And here finally they rode at anchor, the rake of their masts beckoning like a finger to a lad who stood on the threshold of eager venture.

Every hour that I was not in school found me at the wharves watching the loading and the unloading, listening to the talk of sailormen and the rousing chanteys. Aye, they sang them lustily, I can warrant.

> Oh, a Yankee ship comes down the river
> Blow, my bully boys, blow!
> Her yards and masts they shine like silver
> Blow, my bully boys, blow!

Backs bent to work, feet braced, brown arms hauling. The smell of tar on a blackened wharf, of hemp, of bananas rotting in a ship's hold; such smells and sights and sounds formed the background of my childhood.

At this time my best friend was old Messina Clarke. What his age may have been, no one could say. He was known as "old" Messina. The adjective seemed to reach into antiquity. A small man he was, but tough; his eyes had been bleached of color under many suns; wrinkles furrowed his face, and his lower jaw was fringed in a scrub of white beard. He carried a spyglass as some men carry a cane and I never recall seeing him abroad without it.

The old man lived at the foot of my street in a shingled house that was like a hundred others of its day, yet had a sort of sea-going look about it. Perhaps it was the figurehead

Messina Clarke was a small man but tough; his eyes had been bleached of color under many suns; wrinkles furrowed his face, and his lower jaw was fringed in a scrub of white beard.

on the front lawn: a roundish mermaid with cheeks puffed to blow a conch. Perhaps it was the lanterns that hung to starboard and larboard of the door, or the ship models seen through the windows. Maybe it was just that the house sheltered Messina Clarke and so reflected the man who lived inside it. For never was there a brinier salt come to final anchor.

I realize now what it was that attracted the old man to me: he was a talker and I was a listener. We shared a common passion in the sea. As I came to know all his anecdotes by heart, it was a simple matter to put in the word that suggested a new story as the one he was telling drew to a close. And what tales they were! Mutinies under the Southern Cross; a captain swinging from a yard-arm; pirates in the China Sea and opium smuggling off Madagascar; slave runners plying their trade between the Ivory Coast and the South American market; yellow jack and whales, and cannibals and pearls. . . .

The old man had started out in life as a cabin boy on a whaler, rising to the envied position of harpooneer; from that, by slow and logical degrees, boat header, then Chief Mate. Finally, Captain. Thus he brought his adventures to a close, but relived them all from day to day in memory. Once I heard my father refer to him as a "tiresome old man," but to me he was the veritable source of all wisdom. Why, he was like a god who held the winds and storms in answer to his command.

Old Messina taught me all that I ever knew about a ship until I came to sail in one. He showed me how to turn a splice, to tie a score of knots, to shoot the sun and box the compass.   Geography came to life all of a sudden, and places like Zamboanga and Malabar rang as familiar to my ear as Nantucket or Salem.

Holding one of his precious ship models on his knee, old Messina would demand, "What's the longest name of any line aboard, lubber?"

I would wrack my brain, go hot and cold, feel a flush of fever in my cheek as I fished for the proper answer.   The old man's anger was lightning let loose.   The air of the quarter-deck hung about him still.   I would stammer out the first rope that came to mind.

"No it ain't, neither!" he would bellow, shaking his fist under my nose.   "It's the main t'gallant stu'ns'l boom-tricing line.   And don't you fergit it the next time I asks you, or I'll scalp you like a bloomin' cannibule!"

When the *Empress of Asia* on her return from China, carrying a cargo worth five hundred thousand dollars, went down off the Horn with all hands, my father was a ruined man. He was a merchant and the cargo had been his private venture. He never recovered from the blow. A year later, when I was fourteen, he died, leaving my mother and me with scarce enough to keep body and soul together. My mother gave music lessons and finally was forced to take a few paying guests into our home. But even this proved insufficient to our needs. It was up to me to do something to swell the family income.

Naturally I looked toward the sea. My mother, with the memory of the *Empress of Asia* fresh in her mind, begged me not to think of sail. My father had friends among the shipbuilders, so it was upon them that I cast my eye.

Gold had been struck in California. Around the Horn, over mountains and prairies, people were swarming. Ninety-odd thousand of them on the Pacific Coast were clamoring for food, for clothing, for the necessities of existence. The long-neglected shipyards came to life, while new ones sprang up with mushroom growth on the shores of Massachusetts, Maine, and New Hampshire. In the harbor of East Boston there was an unbroken line of yards stretching from Jeffries Point to Chelsea Bridge. Humming with industry they were, in answer to the call of the Gold Coast. Flour was bringing $40.00 a barrel; sugar $4.00 a pound; shoes were selling at $45.00 a pair, and laudanum at $1.00 a drop. The miners could wash from 100 to 1000 dollars worth of gold dust in a day, and often the profits from one voyage of a fast clipper would pay for the original cost of the ship.

At the foot of Border Street, Donald McKay had his
shipyard.   Donald McKay . . . there's magic in the name!
He was a young man at that time; not more than thirty-
seven or -eight, I would say, but already his name was upon
every tongue.   It's the necessities of an age that produce
the men it needs.   Donald McKay was one of those by
whom a period in history is remembered.   John Griffiths of
New York started the ball a-rolling with the *Sea Witch*, the
first true clipper.   Thacher Magown of Mystic River fame
crowded close upon his heels.

But it was McKay who carried shipbuilding onward to
new heights.   Creative artist and master engineer he was;
a dreamer, too, but with the drive of energy to bring his
dreams to reality.   Even the names of his ships quicken the
blood and conjure up a vision before the eye: *Staghound,
Lightning, Westward Ho, Sovereign of the Seas, Flying Cloud*
. . . these were but a few of the sixty or more that stood
to his final credit.

Many times I had heard my father speak of him with
admiration.   Only the old die-hards were set against the
man: turning a ship's bows inside out wasn't natural in a ship,
they maintained.   And at first it looked as if they were right.
The clippers did drive themselves under until their com-
manders learned to crowd most of their canvas on the main
and mizzen.   Then the records began to give the lie to the
old men's croaking.   In Topliff's News Room the Marine
Intelligence column of the *Transcript* published Arrivals and
Clearances that confounded the wiseacres.   China and back
within six months!   Ridiculous.   But true.   Ships that
averaged, if the *Transcript* didn't lie, 15¾ knots an hour.

Well, muttered the die-hards, you couldn't believe everything you saw in print. But the old order was changing. Men were talking speed—speed in terms of dollars.

I determined to try to see Donald McKay. That afternoon as I made my way to Border Street, the wharves were humming with activity despite the biting December air. News had just been signaled from Telegraph Hill that a clipper was in sight, Boston bound. Men were grouped on the street corners, speculating as to her ownership, laying bets on her speed, her cargo. Clerks poked their heads out of countinghouse windows; spyglasses were trained to eastward. It was a scene that I knew and loved. Vessels were moored at the very doors of the warehouses, discharging their cargoes or lading for the far places of the world. Clippers and brigs and barkentines shoved at one another, the arrogant angle of their sprits jutting up across the street as high as the third story of the storehouses. I saw the house-flag of Enoch Train's packets fluttering its white diamond on a red ground. Here was the sea come to meet the land and declare a truce. Here men made ready to have their business upon the great waters.

I hurried along Border Street, past Central Square. There they were—the McKay yards! I turned in at the entrance to a fenced-in area and my ear was assailed by the whir of saws, the ring of axes, the fused sounds of wood and metal in the shaping. A smell of fresh-sawed pine and oak smote my nostrils. Outside the frame building that housed Donald McKay's drafting room and mold loft, I paused. It took some courage to enter. Once inside it wasn't so bad. I looked at the stool perchers bent over their ledgers, and took heart. Pale men they were, existing on the salt edge of adventure. Nothing scary about *them.*

The prestige of my father's name turned the trick. I was permitted to climb a narrow wooden stair leading to the drafting room above. The sanctum sanctorum. I lifted my fist to knock. I stopped. Behind that door Donald McKay was at work. I realized that I was trembling. Swallowing hard, I thumped the panel.

"Come in!" boomed a voice.

I opened the door and entered. In the gloom of the vast room all I could see for a moment was the square of light where the window gave on the shipyards. A man was bent over a drafting table. My eyes, accustoming themselves to the gloom, took in many things at once. A high-ceilinged room with rows of shelves lining the walls; in a far corner a cherry-bellied stove glowed to defeat the outer chill. There was a clutter of nautical paraphernalia everywhere: a model clipper with false gunports painted along her sides; a mounted shark whose slim hull was marked off in geometric sections; samples of copper and wood and sailcloth; whale-oil lamps above the drafting table; a set of bellows worked by pedals that could create a miniature wind of hurricane hazard from any point of the compass; wooden lift-models and mechanical drawings; many strange sea-going devices that would have baffled a landlubber.

I started to speak, then stopped. My attention had been caught and riveted by the model of a ship cradled in its wooden brace. Clean-lined and eager as a greyhound she was; no trailboards, no cathead carving, no ornamental barnacles of any sort. She had the lean belly of a sprinter, and from the sudden sharpness of her stem the figure of an angel rose with trumpet poised, like a herald of good tidings; and in the uprush of the figure I could almost hear the ringing gladness of the trumpet blast! Here was the core and essence of a ship, a ship to carry herself with pride before the wind. From truck to keel, from rudderpost to jib boom, she was a miracle of proportion and grace. In the shaft of cold sunlight that slanted through the window she seemed almost to breathe, and I caught my own breath in wonder.

I felt as if all the sinews of my body had been plucked by an unseen hand and set a-humming, as a vessel's cordage hums to a sudden-bursting gale. I wanted to shout and sing, but my tongue was silent. Only a model of a ship. But enough. She was beauty moving toward perfection.

Thus I first saw the *Flying Cloud*.

Aye, as if it were yesterday, I remember that moment. Perhaps destiny, hovering above our heads, sweeps close enough sometimes for us to feel the brush of its wing. I knew that this ship and my life were to be bound up together, come what might.

"Weel, young lad, an' what might ye be after?"

The voice of the man at the drafting table brought me back with a start. A flavor of the hielands hung about his speech, like a smell of heather blown across a moor. I saw a stocky man, ruddy colored, with thick, black hair growing after its own impulse. His mouth was firm, even stern; his eyes direct and piercing; his chin square and deep-cleft.

My throat felt tight and my voice small, but I remember the friendliness that sparked his eyes as he glanced across the drawing table at me.

Turning back to me, Donald McKay demanded, "An' what mak's ye come to me for a position?"

"I—I want a position, sir."

"An' what can ye do?"

"I can draw ships, too," came my answer, with courage mustered from somewhere.

He laughed then. "Hoot! An' that's a braw deeclaration! What's yer name?"

"Enoch Thacher."

"Son of Joel Thacher, the merchant?"

When I nodded in the affirmative, he said: "I knew yer faither weel, laddie. A fine mon he was, too." His mouth relaxed into a smile and I felt my heart grow warm toward him.

Donald McKay turned and laid his hand upon the ship model that had cast a spell over me. For a moment he was silent.

"I caught ye lookin' upon this ship," he said at last. His eyes lighted and he moved his fingers over the model with a sculptor's touch. "Up New York way they're sayin' that we Doon Easters canna' build ships to outsail theirs. Weel— they can tak' a round turn out o' theirsel's and go to Tophet! I ken that this sweet lassie will mak' them eat their words. She'll be as quick in light airs as in a howlin' blaw, or I'm a Dutchman. Look-ye how I've sharpened her bows and flattened her forebody, and peeled her under the counters! She'll hold to a maximum o' speed wi'out drivin' hersel' under. An' as for they newfangled teapots that run wi' engines!" He gave a snort of disgust and patted the model almost with reverence. "The end o' sail, the wise oracles are sayin'. Just wait till *you* tak' to water, my pet!" Turning back toward me, he demanded, "An' what mak's ye come to me for a position?"

"Well, sir," I stammered, "I often heard my father speak of you as—as a man of genius, sir. And I've loved ships ever since I was born." I was twisting my hat and wondering why I had been cursed with such a clumsy tongue.

Donald McKay looked at me with those piercing eyes that could have found out the flaw in any living thing.

"So ye love ships, eh?" he chuckled. "I mind when I was yer age I loved them too. Grand fun it was to be a-straddle a skys'l yard, swaying to the pitchin' o' the ship. Sometimes as I sit here on the land, designin' ships for other men tae sail, I think aboot it, an' remember the gales an' the storms. An' I tell ye, it mak's a shiver run through the marrow o' my bones! Ye ken, laddie, there are men this world who ne'er see a drop o' water but what they wash in? To them the sea is an auld wife's tale wi'out muckle o' truth to it. But for men like you an' me, laddie, it's a braw sight, an' ane that plucks at yer heart wi' cold fingers. Bonnie, but awesome." His eyes had the look of a man who sees a vision, and I held my breath lest I break the spell.

Donald McKay turned back toward his work. "All right, laddie," he said abruptly, "I'll sign ye on. Three dollars a week, an' mind ye spend it cannily. Nip awa' home noo, an' report tomorrow."

I was dismissed. I could only stammer my thanks as I backed toward the door and stumbled over the boot scraper. My mind churned with the things I had seen and heard and felt. In a stride Donald McKay had taken his place beside Messina Clarke as one of the gods of my childhood. But there was a pivot, a focal point, around which even he

whirled as a minor impression, as they say a satellite whirls about an orb of greater magnitude: the *Flying Cloud* . . .

Out in the street again I stood stock-still before McKay's office, stood there like one daft, and stared up at his window, through which I could see the top of his head as he bent over his work. The *Flying Cloud!* To work all day within hand's reach of her. To see her taking shape as one week merged into another, expanding, growing to the fulfilment of her perfection. To have a part, no matter how small, in her creation.

The gold of that wintry late afternoon was round about me. The striking of the old South Church bell reached my ear across the clear air. The sea was as blue as an oath.

I felt suddenly charged with resolution and purpose. A knight of old seeing a vision of the Grail could have known no more solemn consecration than did I.

For the *Flying Cloud*, I vowed I would give the best that was in me: my strength, my youth, my life if need be!

CHAPTER II

A Ship Is Born

AS I HURRIED homeward, I could scarce contain myself. I wanted to shout and jump for joy. A job in Donald McKay's shipyard! To work all day within sight of the water; to see ships come and go, and to earn three dollars a week!

The wind had risen and the bite of it sent my chin deeper within my greatcoat collar. Sparrows huddled on the roof tops, like Millerites awaiting the call to Judgment. First I must tell my good news to old Messina Clarke. I found him chipping the ice off his front walk, without hat or overcoat. He was as tough as a length of new hemp, and he wielded a rusty hoe with as much vigor as if he were bending sail in the teeth of a nor'easter.

"Cap'n! Cap'n Clarke!" I shouted. "I got it!"

"Got wot?" he grunted.

"Got a job, Cap'n!"

He set down the hoe then and looked up. "Where?"

"With Donald McKay," I bragged. "You know—the man whose clippers they're all talking about."

"Humph, McKay!" growled old Messina, with a sour look.

"Well, don't you want to hear about it?" I demanded, angling to be invited into the warmth of his study. There a fire was sure to be burning on the hearth and there, I knew, the old man would brew a pot of coffee strong enough to fell a bucko mate.

Without answering, old Messina turned to enter the house. This was his invitation. Otherwise he would have roared, "Home with ye, ye blitherin' coot, or I'll lay a marlinespike around yer ears!"

Once inside the narrow study, I threw off my beaver cap and shrugged out of my greatcoat. Here I felt at home, and here I had passed the happiest hours of my life. In one corner stood the revolving globe on which I had traced the course of all the old man's voyages. Over the mantle hung a model of the Indiaman *Aeolus*, last of his commands. Beautifully carved and finished in each detail she was, with gold leaf laid on below the water line in place of copper; the pride of the old man's heart. Three years he had given to the making of her. Maps hung about the walls, and trophies from every corner of the world: headdresses of human hair from the Marquesas; stone gods from the Solomons; whalebone fashioned into strange objects.

Tables and chairs were piled with books over which I had spent long hours in attempting to master such rudiments of navigation as my brain could encompass. In this room I had labored to solve the riddle of Napierian logarithms in order to follow the tables in Bowditch.

"Well," growled old Messina, dumping a half pound of coffee into a pot and stirring it up furiously with a broken egg and some water, "I'm a-waitin'."

Here I felt at home and here I had passed the happiest hours of my life . . . .
Tables and chairs were piled with books over which I had spent long hours in
attempting to master such rudiments of navigation as my brain could encompass.

"Well," I began, "I went to see McKay because Father used to say that he was the only man who was one jump ahead——" I got no further.

"McKay!" the old man snorted. "Young upstart, that's what he is!"

I leaped to the defense of my new god. "Why do you say that?" I demanded.

Old Messina stared at me for a moment in amazement. "Why do I say that?" he mimicked sarcastically. Not often had I challenged his judgment. "Didn't I stop in at his office one fine day to look at his precious models? 'Ye're puttin' a stem like a bowie knife on them-there ships,' I says to him. 'Tain't natural in a ship.' And what, thinks you, he answers me back?"

"What, Cap'n," I muttered, subdued by now.

The old man changed his voice into a genteel imitation of McKay's speech. "'The East Indiaman has had its day,' says he to me. 'These clipper bows that I design will achieve a maximum o' speed.' 'Tain't the shape o' yer bows that'll beat them steam paddle boxes,' I says to him, 'It's brains on the quarter-deck.' 'It's both, Cap'n,' says he; 'give me quarter-deck brains and my designs and together we'll trim them all.' That's what he says to me. To *me* that was born on a passage around the Horn. I've wrung more salt water out o' my socks that ever he sailed on!" Messina spat his scorn. "Bows turned inside out that way," he muttered. "She'll bury herself in the first ground swell!"

Old Messina, you may observe, was one of the die-hards. Even when the *Sea Witch* made the record passage of 97 days to 'Frisco the old man had refused to credit it.

Old Messina Clarke.

"Anyway," I ventured, "McKay is going to pay me three dollars a week, and maybe he'll let me draw ships, too."

"*Draw* ships!" Messina exploded. "It's high time you was a-sailin' 'em!"

Needless to say I was disappointed in the way the old man received my good news. For the first time I felt that he had failed me. It didn't occur to me then that it might be a blow to him to see me turning to someone else for nautical training.

My mother took it differently. "Donald McKay is a splendid man and he was a good friend of your father's. You mustn't mind what old Messina says. He's a little touchy, you know. I think it's a wonderful opportunity, but I shall be thankful if the association doesn't lead you into sailing."

The fact that I must leave school to make my own way in the world did not upset me. What school could have rivaled the interest of the surroundings in which I now found myself? From six o'clock in the morning till six at night I labored over a drawing table in the mold loft of Donald McKay's shipyard.

My work in the beginning, in all truth, was elementary enough: I was allowed to trace the simpler details of ornament for the great-cabin. Today I realize that it was only the kindness of his heart for the son of a friend that prompted McKay to take me into his office. In those first weeks, if the destiny of the ship and the fate of all who manned her had been dependent upon my efforts, I could not have felt a greater sense of responsibility.

Through our offices filed a procession of shipwrights, chandlers, underwriters, lumbermen, engineers, sailmakers, captains active and retired. I kept my eyes upon my work, for McKay was a hard taskmaster, but I kept my ears apeak, and they missed no detail of all that there was to hear.

Donald McKay not only designed his ships, he superintended their construction as well. When he first began to build, it was the custom to hack frame timbers out of the rough with a broadax; when a timber must be cut lengthwise, it was sawed through by hand, a laborious process and

a slow one. Here McKay showed the independence of his mind by setting up a sawmill in his yards to do both these jobs. It was an innovation, I can tell you. The saw hung in a mechanical contraption in such way that the workmen could control the tilt of it and thus get the desired bevel of cut. Once men had had to carry the big timbers on their shoulders; McKay erected a steam derrick to do it for them. It caused a lot of amusement among the scoffers but did the same work in jig time.

So active had the New England shipbuilders become that the seaboard forests were being stripped bare of timber. Men had to look farther for wood. McKay met this problem after his own fashion: he made a full set of patterns for every stick and timber in his ships; these patterns were taken into the northern forests during the winter; lumberjacks felled trees of the necessary number and size. Then over snow and ice the logs were hauled to the rivers before the spring thaws, and down in East Boston his adzes and hammers and his caulking irons rang to high heaven.

Sometimes the poet Longfellow dropped in to pass the time of day. If old Messina hadn't always snorted at poets and suchlike, I might have paid more attention to Longfellow. But I do remember that after a visit to our yards, he once wrote a poem about a launching, and Donald McKay tacked a copy of it up on the wall of the mold loft. Probably it has never come to your eye, since they tell me that these enlightened days of the twentieth century hold Longfellow something of a fogy with a goodly coating of moss to his back. Maybe so. Anyway, here is the stanza:

Then the Master,
With a gesture of command,
Waved his hand;
And at the word,
Loud and sudden there was heard,
All around them and below,
The sound of hammers, blow on blow,
Knocking away the shores and spurs.
And see! she stirs!
She starts—she moves—she seems to feel
The thrill of life along her keel.

Not bad for a poet, moss or no moss. Once Richard Henry Dana, who wrote *Two Years Before the Mast*, stopped by for a chat with Donald McKay: a quiet, studious-looking man he was, with little look of the sea about him. Aye, it was all-absorbing to a lad like me, you can imagine.

Up in the mold loft the air was charged with activity. Draftsmen, down on their knees, drew diagonals and trapezoids in chalks on the floor. No one but a shipwright could have made head nor tail to them. McKay hovered over his men like a hawk, his keen eyes catching out any error of workmanship. With mammoth calipers he checked every line that the draftsmen drew, and they trembled lest the master find so much as a quarter-inch difference in their renderings of his plans. Sometimes he paced the floor as we worked, and you knew by the far look in his eyes that he was seeing this ship full-bodied and in her element—the sea. Now and again he'd halt, study the sheaf of plans in his hand, then bend to chalk a correction in the designs on the floor.

Every important timber in the ship—and there were more than two hundred—had been drawn in small scale on these plans. The draftsmen redrew them in chalk on the floor, some fifty times larger. Though the mold loft was 100 feet long by 150 feet deep, it was not vast enough to accommodate all these great drawings; they overlapped and crisscrossed until they would have seemed a Chinese puzzle to a landsman's eye.

So the *Flying Cloud* took shape. First the seed which germinated in one man's mind; then the model by which lesser men could catch the vision of her; then the mechanical drawings that put her into figures of geometry and conic sections. But as I labored there from daylight till dusk, bent over my drafting table and completely happy, those drawings became more in my sight than intersecting arcs and geometric trapezoids: they were the yards and spars of my ship, buffeted by the gales of the Roaring Forties, and I was athwart the t'gallant yard with my feet hooked into the lifts, fisting sail in the teeth of a heroic wind!

It was a great day when the converter was given the order to make his molds. It meant that at last the *Flying Cloud* was emerging from her chrysalis of drafting paper into tangible form. The converter and his men moved into the loft, puffed up with the sense of their own importance. First they cut thin deal boards into molds, each one of which followed exactly the shape of the chalk drawings on the loft floor. Then as fast as each mold was cut, it was carried off to the neighboring lumberyard where Donald McKay himself picked out timbers of the proper grain and size and marked each one with the number of its mold.

Pileheads had been driven deep into the slip to form a bed for the ship to rest upon. Timbers were laid horizontal-wise across the pileheads. On rugged blocks of oak along the center of the groundways the backbone of the vessel had its beginning. Of solid rock maple were her keel timbers; next, the upward thrust of her stempiece curved from its boxing into the keel; the sternpost was set in its mortise, while amidships the white-oak ribs swelled and rounded.

Fortunately it was a mild winter and no weather was so bad as to keep the men from their appointed jobs. From

light till dark the yards hummed with activity. The saws whirred; the derrick groaned its complaint; adze and caulking iron kept up their resounding clamor, while the air was filled with the tang of fresh sawed oak and pine. Wood powder drifted like mist from the pits where the under-sawyers worked; the fires of the blacksmiths glowed in the wind.

In those days men took a pride in their work. The humblest apprentice in the yards seemed to feel that he was engaged upon a great, aye, even a sacred undertaking. For

them the *Flying Cloud* was not just one more ship; she was timber and iron springing into life under their hands. Funny thing—that sense of the reality of a ship which impresses itself upon those who have a hand in her shaping. There was not a workman in the yards who doubted that a living spirit was housed within his handiwork. Just so the sailor believes that it's the soul of a ship which makes an individual of her. And who can declare that they're wrong? It is a fact that two ships built after the same plans, in the same yards, by the identical builder, will display wide-differing qualities when they take to sea. The one will prove herself

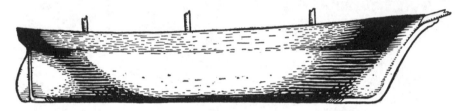

in a gale; the other in light airs. One will be a killer of men on every passage while the other will never start a sheet or lose a spar. No one can deny that such differences exist. Your landsman will declare that it is some slight variation in line of hull or rake of mast or hang of canvas. But the landsman knows naught about these things. The sailor, living close to the elements, understands much that never meets the eye.

The winter months passed. Spring made itself felt in the mildness of the air. Now we could throw open the windows of the drafting room, and the water in the harbor was softer to the eye. The *Flying Cloud* lay on her strait bed at the water's edge, grown past all recognition of her beginnings. Nigh a million feet of splendid white oak with scantlings of southern pine had gone into her frame, and over fifty tons of copper, exclusive of sheathing. She was seasoned with salt and "tuned" like a Stradivarius. Duncan MacLane wrote in the Boston *Atlas:* "Hers is the sharpest bow we have ever seen on any ship." Men were laying bets on her potential speed, investing their life savings in her cargo. A ship built by Donald McKay to better the record of the *Staghound—* they couldn't lose!

Each night on my way homeward I would stop in for a chat with Messina Clarke. While the old man pretended indifference to McKay's newfangled methods of building, he was consumed by curiosity. I know

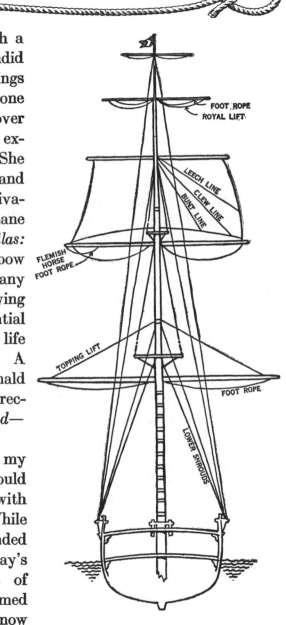

now, too, that he resented this new world of mine in which he could not wholly share.

After devious circlings, old Messina would arrive at the point he wanted to know. Clearing his throat, he would ask:

"And what might the rake of her masts be, lubber?"

"Alike they're one-and-one-quarter inches to the foot," I would answer.

"Humph!" came his snort. "She'll lose her sticks in the first good blow, mark my words!"

Silence. Then: "And what might the finish of her great-cabin be?" he would question.

"She's wainscoted with satinwood, mahogany, and rose-wood, set off with enameled pilasters, and cornices of gilt work."

"By the horns o' Satan!" he roared. His indignation was boundless. "Plain pine with a coat o' white lead was good enough for my day! Ships was meant to be ships, as men was meant to be men. Whoever did see a man with his hair curled and scent to his coat what was worth a chip on a millrace? Dressin' a ship up like that! It's—it's indecent!"

But despite his scorn, no part of the development of the *Flying Cloud* escaped his attention or comment. Together we had watched her grow from a tadpole into a whale; keel and rib, floor plank and monkey rail, stem and steering post. I, from the drafting room, where I could see every stick and timber as it swung into place on the stocks, and old Messina seeing it all in my accounts of each day's activity. For us both the *Flying Cloud* stood for much more than a

ship: for me she was a symbol of romance and eager venture;
of the mysterious lands that lay beyond the ocean's rim; of
things longed for and hopes fulfilled. For the old man she
was all that the sea stood for in his salty mind; his boyhood;
the vasty ventures of his middle years; sunlight and whistling gale.

It was with a feeling of sorrow that we watched each
day bringing her nearer completion, as one regrets seeing
a babe emerge into a child, child into man. Every handspike hammered into her hull came to echo dully in our ears.
We resented the cocky air of the workmen who acted
as if the *Cloud* were their ship when we knew her to be ours
alone.

Inevitably there came a day when the last trunnel had
been driven, when the whang of mallet and adze was silent,
and the whir of the saws had stilled. The figurehead, wrapped
about in cotton swathings, was hoisted to its mortise and
bolted into place. There was a hush, like a portent. So
it might be in the moment before a giant awakes. The
Flying Cloud, all glistening black and copper, lay at the
water's edge, alive, eager, straining for the sea. It was her
time to go. Her destiny must be fulfilled.

On April 15, 1851, she was launched. Not long
ago I came across a yellowed clipping in my sea chest
that will give you a better picture of the event than words of
mine:

"The ceremony of introducing the noble fabric to her
watery home occurred in the presence of an immense crowd
of spectators, and she passed to her mission on the deep amid
the roar of cannon and the cheers of the people. Visitors

The *Flying Cloud*, all glistening black and copper, lay at the water's edge, aliv

eager, straining for the sea.   It was her time to go.   Her destiny must be fulfilled.

were in town from the back country and from along the coast
to witness the launch, particularly from Cape Cod, delega-
tions from which arrived by the morning train.   The wharves
on both sides the stream, where a view was attainable, were
thronged with people.   Men, women, and children vied with
one another to get a look; and men and boys clung like
spiders to the rigging of the ships and the sides and roofs of
stores and houses, to get a glance at this magnificent vessel.
As the hammer of the clock fell at 12, the stroke of a gun
at the shipyard announced that the ship had started on her
ways, and she pursued her graceful course to the arms of the
loving wave that opened wide to receive her . . ."

Aye, it was a great day for us all.   Donald McKay,
with hollows under his sleepless eyes, watched the launch
from a window in his office.   As the ship slid down her tal-
lowed ways and came to the staging's end, the slash of a
knife freed the figurehead of its cotton wrappings, and an
exclamation went up from the spectators in a vast sigh.
The figure of an angel seemed to float on outspread wings,
rising slenderly out of the stem, while the sun struck against
the gold of the trumpet at her lips like a ringing cry of
triumph.

For myself, I knew only a feeling of sorrow as my ship
took to water.   As soon as her masts were stepped, she was
to be towed away to New York.   Grinnell, Minturn & Company of that city had purchased her from Enoch Train for
$90,000.   A sale which, be it said in passing, Enoch Train
was never to cease regretting, although the croakers shook
their heads in gloomy prediction that Grinnell was sailing
both sheets aft for bankruptcy.

I doubted that I should ever lay eyes upon my ship again. No matter how many vessels I might see turned out of the McKay yards, no other would mean so much to me. She was my first love; puppy love, some thoughtless ones call it. No other love strikes its grappling hook so deep into the heart.

It was some weeks later, wnen the *Cloud's* masts had been stepped and the riggers had done their work, that the tug *Ajax* nosed into the harbor. I wanted to shout out my protest! I hoped the tug might ram a rock and sink, and the Captain fall to a watery grave, and all the men be stricken with paralysis! None of these dire events came to pass. The *Ajax* meant business and she set about it.

As the *Flying Cloud* was towed out to sea, I stood on the hill behind Messina Clarke's house, beside the towering figure-head, and wondered how the mermaid could blow her conch on such a mournful day.

". . . They placed a silver coin under the heel of your mainmast step, *Flying Cloud*, to speed you on long voyages. Storms are waiting for you, and seas to batter you. Davy Jones will reach for you and every skeleton in his locker will rattle its bones. But there are spice islands in another sea, waiting for you, *Flying Cloud*. Only I won't be there . . ."

And then I turned away, for I was a big lad by now, going on fifteen, and mighty near to blubbering.

"Cap'n," I muttered, turning back to the old man, "Cap'n——" then stopped. For Messina Clarke, with the back of one hoary fist, was knuckling a tear out of his own eye!

Since that day, so long ago now, I have come to learn that there is no heart so soft as the sailorman's, and none more filled with sentiment. Stout hearts, but never hard ones. So we stood there, under a gilded mermaid, an old man and a boy watching a ship being towed out to sea.

What was passing in the old man's mind, I can never know. For myself, I felt that I had lost a friend.

CHAPTER III

The Unforeseen Happens—I Go to Sea

ALONG South Street, New York, the wharves stretched out into the East River like the fingers of a hand. From below Wall Street, as far up as Market and Pike streets, a forest of masts lifted tall and straight against the sky. If you were seaman enough to be able to tell one ship from another, you could have made out brigs, barques, barkentines, clippers, East Indiamen, packets of the famous Black Ball Line, sturdy whalers out of Nantucket, Flemish luggers, and French *corvettes*. The eager thrust of their bowsprits, pointing up across the street, all but raked the shuttered windows of the warehouses. Ships from every harbor of the world, lading their cargoes of cotton and potash and flour or disgorging their chests of fragrant tea, bales of Chinese silks, hogsheads of sugar, and puncheons of rum.

South Street belonged to the sea. The signs of the ship chandlers swung in the breeze. Windows displayed quadrants, compasses, and barometers, and all manner of sea-going gear. There were sail lofts, and the houses of the underwriters, merchants, and auctioneers. Thus the commerce of the continent met the trade of the ocean in a bustle of activity that deafened the ear and confused the eye.

Pier 20 was a blackened wharf whose cobbles rumbled with drays, horses, barrows, and toiling men. Here lay a ship whose masts towered out of all proportion to wise practice. The sun shone smartly on her yards and gleaming brightwork; on the lines of pins in the pinrails; on the gold of the figurehead growing out of the upward curve of her stem. Her hull was charged with the lean tension of a greyhound, and from her foremast a canvas tarpaulin flaunted the legend:

FOR SAN FRANCISCO
CLIPPER *FLYING CLOUD*
APPLY GRINNELL, MINTURN & COMPANY

While at the maintruck the swallow-tailed house flag of red, blue, and yellow fluttered in the ocean-wandering breeze. From somewhere about her decks a man's voice was singing:

O! A sailor's life is the life for me!
A gallant barque and a roarin' sea!
Ho—my bullies, yo ho!

A clipper had arrived that morning from the Orient, the first of the season's China tea racers. The smell of her cargo lay fragrant on the air; tea of the first picking it was, from Whampoa. Merchants were swarming around her like flies about a honeypot. Bids were soaring. The finest teas had a way of molding in the salt air of a long sea voyage; hence the first and swiftest clipper home fetched top prices for her cargo.

A Chinese mandarin, passenger on the newly arrived ship, drew his brocaded robes about him and disappeared

in a lurching carriage.   Sailors ashore rubbed elbows with
sea captains; country folk, in to see the sights of the great
city, gazed with like astonishment at coolies and crimps
and boarding-house runners.   A restless place was South
Street in 1851, I can tell you; as humming with industry as a
beehive.   Manhattan was an island who had her business
with the sea; there was no question about that.

My eyes took in every detail of the scene, as a hungry
man might look upon a table laden with good food.   The
ring of the chanteys and the click-click of capstan were
music to my ears.   A polyglot of ship smells that every
sailor knows struck me like a blow; made up it was of Stock-
holm tar and bilge and rotting fruit and moldering cargo,
cut through by a reek of fish.   Yet it was as sweet as the
perfumes of Araby!   The harbor at East Boston had a like
smell, and it made me, for the moment, less homesick.

My sea chest, brass-bound and nautical as you please,
lay in a humble room of the Seaman's Rest.   It held my
purchases of duck pants, woolen underwear, oilskins, sea
boots, my precious spyglass, together with sundry incidentals
that the clerk had persuaded me that Jack always took to sea.

That morning in the Grinnell offices, producing the
letter from Donald McKay that was the opening wedge, I
had signed my Indentures, thereby agreeing faithfully to
serve my employers for a period of two years; to discharge
my duties to the best of my meager ability; to obey my
officers; not to embezzle my ship's goods; not to frequent
saloons or play at games of chance!   In consideration for
which service, the shipowners did contract to teach the
"undersigned Apprentice the whole business of being a

seaman . . . and to provide same with sufficient food and drink . . ."

I'm sure you've known all along, my good reader, that I was to sail on the *Flying Cloud.* Well—I did. It came about like this: Two weeks after the *Ajax* had towed the *Cloud* out of Boston Harbor, Donald McKay had stopped before my drafting table one morning and remarked:

"What's ailin' ye, laddie. Ye're as uneasy as a bear on a hot griddle."

"Why—nothing, sir."

"Nothin', eh? I'll wager I could mak' a sharp guess! Couldna' by any chance be the *Cloud,* could it?"

I glanced up to see him looking at me with a shrewd twinkle in his eye.

"Is there news of her, sir?" I cried. "Has she arrived in New York? When is she sailing?'

He sat down opposite me then, and it struck me that I had seldom seen him unbend to this degree.

"Aye, she's arrived, right enough," he assented. "Berthed up snug as a bug at Pier 20. They're stowin' her for the trip around the Horn to California and thence to China." Donald McKay leaned across the table. "An' how would ye like tae sail aboord her, laddie? Afore the mast?"

The question was a quiet one but it struck my ear like a pistol shot.

"Muckle ye ken aboot ships now," the man continued, "but it's a' theory. Ye can name every inch o' cordage, but I'll warrant ye'd hae a deal o' trouble pickin' them oot in the teeth o' a nor'easter. There's but one way to *know* ships, laddie, an' that's tae sail them. Yer friend Cap'n Clarke would fall in wi' that, albeit he doesna' hold wi' a lot o' my views."

Sail on the *Cloud!* I could scarce breathe for the feelings that whirled through me.

"I've talked wi' Grinnell's aboot ye," the man was saying, "an' if ye mak' a favorable impression they will sign ye on. Likewise I spoke wi' yer guid mother an' explained tae her that if ye would be a fine shipbuilder ye've got tae come up through the hawsepipe an' not in at the cabin window. She has confidence in me and gi'ed her consent."

"My mother—consented?"

Donald McKay nodded. He stood up then and laid his hands on my shoulders with firm grip.

"Think weel before ye mak' yer decision. An' sleep on it too," he warned. "I would ne'er advise any man tae tak' up a seafarin' life save as a means tae an end. Hard it is, an' cruel an' dangerous; small pay in it an' smaller future. Yer womenfolk will wring oot their hearts wi' weepin' for ye. Aye, a hard school, an' no mistake! So think aboot it, lad, an' if ye decide upon this step, yer wages can be paid each month tae yer mother, an' yer mind can be at ease aboot her."

"There's nothing I would rather do than sail aboard the *Cloud*, sir," I managed finally.

He chuckled. "I had an idea 'twas so! Talk it over wi' yer mother, laddie, an' mak' up your mind. An' if ye should decide the way I think ye will, may God go wi' ye."

When I reached home, I found my mother in the parlor with old Messina sitting to one side of the stove, drawing on

his pipe. There was an air of expectancy, as if portentous things were about to happen. My mother looked up as I entered and I saw that her eyes were bright. She dropped her needlework and crossed to my side.

Before I could speak, she exclaimed: "You are going to sea in the *Flying Cloud!* My dear son, how glad I—am!" She kissed me, and if her heart was nigh to breaking, her voice was soft and sure.

Messina Clarke rose with creaking bones and came over to me. "You've the makin' of a deep-sea sailor in you, lad," he said huskily, putting his hands on my shoulders, "and so I've been a-tellin' your mother. I've watched you ever since you was a little tyke buildin' ships out o' seegar boxes and riggin' 'em with string, and sailin' 'em in every puddle 'twixt here and Bunker Hill. The sea's the place for the likes o' you. Contrary to that McKay upstart, you'll ne'er spend your days in any office when once you've felt the lift of a deck under your feet! 'Tis the only life fit for a man. Blast me, if I wasn't so blamed rusty in the j'ints, I'd ship aboard the *Cloud* myself. She'll need a proper salt-water sailor on her with her bows blown inside out thataways!"

"If only he were a little older," sighed my mother.

"Older?" queried Messina testily. "He's fifteen, ain't he? The sooner a man gits started about his business in life the better, I say."

I couldn't speak, for the life of me. I glanced around the room at the familiar objects that I had lived with all my life and never really seen until this moment: the hair flowers under a glass protector on the mantle; the framed sampler worked by my mother when she was a child—*Abigail*

I kissed my mother good-by, and she clung to me. Her lips whispered
against my ear, "God keep you, my son, and bring you home."

Winthrop, Aged Seven; a painting of the ill-starred *Empress of Asia;* silhouettes and whatnots. . . . Now that I was leaving, they had a meaning.

So it was settled. I was to drive by coach to New York, an event that under ordinary circumstances would have been a big adventure; but with a passage around the Horn in the *Flying Cloud* in the offing, it seemed little enough.

The next few days sped by like a dream. When an evening came that the coach drew up to the door, my carpet-bag was packed in readiness with a few belongings: a fresh shirt, underwear; a muffler of thickest wool knitted by my mother (though the month was May)—"for the weather you will meet off Cape Horn," she said—a brass spyglass from Messina Clarke, his best one, too; and lastly, a box of sandwiches and my favorite cakes.

I kissed my mother good-by, and she clung to me. Her lips whispered against my ear, "God keep you, my son, and bring you home."

I threw up my head, for I was a sailor and I was going to sea.

Old Messina gripped my arms. "Remember, boy," he muttered, "when you're down there off the Horn: one hand for yourself and one for the ship. Never forget! One hand for yourself and one for the ship!"

Good old Messina. Little did I suspect that when a day came that I should be in East Boston once more, you would be gone. Rest in peace, old friend, in Fiddler's Green where the ghosts of all good sailormen keep their watch below. But for you, how different would the course of my life have run.

I was past speech and must have looked mighty glum, for old Messina cried, "Brail up, lubber!" and fetched me a crack on the back, then came about and blew his nose violently. I stumbled across the sidewalk to the waiting coach. The door banged behind me. A whip cracked—the horses strained forward in their harness. Then the darkness shut down and I remember only the lurching, lurching of the coach on the highway to New York.

*   *   *   *   *   *   *   *

The *Flying Cloud* was to sail with the afternoon tide. Stevedores struggled up one gangplank to descend by another. They had finished lading the lower hold, and a diminishing pile of cargo on the wharf showed that their work 'tweendecks was almost done. The mates were standing over them, bawling orders. A ticklish business, this stowing of cargo, since the *Cloud* was as yet an untried ship and the lading must balance her sail plan.

By twelve noon I went aboard my ship with the sea chest aperch my shoulder. My lubber's clothes were stored in the bottom of it against the day—who knew when—I should step back once more upon native soil. In my new rig I felt that I would pass muster as an old sea dog: blue shirt, duck trousers tight around the midriff and falling loose about the feet; a varnished hat with its dangling "admiral's pennant"; a black silk neckerchief, and lastly a nautical-looking knife slung with importance to my belt. Little did I realize that complexion and walk removed me at a glance from confusion with the seasoned sailormen who swung down the decks with bronzed cheek and rolling gait. I lowered my brass-bound sea chest and looked about. How the long

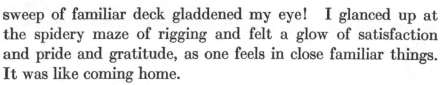
sweep of familiar deck gladdened my eye! I glanced up at the spidery maze of rigging and felt a glow of satisfaction and pride and gratitude, as one feels in close familiar things. It was like coming home.

Perhaps a man's fate is written when he is born—and a ship's too. . . . "I knew that it was my fate to cross your wake, *Flying Cloud!* You didn't think you could clear for China without me, did you? I can hear the water chuckling about your forefoot and the song of the ropes running through your blocks. What are you telling me? That the wind blows fresh, and there are spice islands on the other side of the——"

"Ahoy, lad! What might you want?" A big man in a blue pea-jacket bore down upon me.

"I'm an apprentice, sir."

"Now whoever would ha' guessed that! Well, I'm the second mate. Mister Andrews to the likes o' you. See that you step smart when I speak or there'll be trouble 'tween you and me." He pointed for'ard along the deck. "Half deck's up there. Stow yerself and yer gear, and brisk about it, too!"

The half deck is the apprentices' quarters. It may be anywhere on a ship except under the foc'sle head. In the *Flying Cloud* it was placed well for'ard and its dignified name gave small indication of its appearance. To the eye it was no more than a scuttle, seen from the deck side. Once below the scuttle you would have found two small boxlike rooms, one of which was fitted with four bunks, the other with six. I turned into the "box" on the starboard side, and by the light that filtered in through the small port I could distinguish four bunks, two on each wall. This, unless something

By twelve noon I went aboard my ship with the sea chest aperch my shoulder.

unforeseen changed the course of planned events was to be my home for the next two years.

The room was half filled with a clutter of ropes, sail-cloth, kindling, pots and pans, and general rubbish. It appeared to be a repository for any odd thing that no other place could be found for. It was completely cheerless. I cleared a space large enough to set down my sea chest, then I sat upon it and took in my surroundings with a dejected eye. I thought of old Messina and his friendly study, of my mother, and in that moment I was no stout-hearted sailorman, I can tell you. But my bleak thoughts were broken by the door banging open. A young lad about my own age bounded into the room.

"My name's Archie Warner," he threw at me by way of greeting. "What's yours?"

I told him. "Are you an apprentice, too?" I queried.

"Aye, and there's two more of us to come in here. Ever been to sea before?"

"No."

"Ho! A proper landlubber, eh? It'll be keelhauling for you, my bucko."

"Well, I can name every line and stay and plank aboard," I bragged.

"Humph!" he grunted. "Bet I can turn a quicker splice than you can!"

"Prove it!"

In no time we were at it, and that's how we became friends. He *could* turn a quicker splice than I, for I have always been clumsy at the trick, but I could beat him all to hollow on the topmast rigging. He was a New Yorker by birth, and the only sailing he had ever done was around the harbor and neighboring waters. He was as tall as I and as hard as a hickory nut; his face was a mask of freckles and his hair as red as a brick. Indeed, that's the name he was soon known by—Brick Warner.

The third and fourth occupants of our cabin appeared. Brick and I examined them with interest. Having been established in our quarters for some fifteen minutes, we felt their seniors and superiors. Their names were Tad Lancraft and Jake Whittlesy; names which were quickly shortened to Lanny and Whit, and as such they were known thereafter.

Lanny was a big lad of sixteen, a full fathom tall. His hands protruded to some length from the ends of his sleeves. In fact the whole impression of him was of being too big for his clothes. He had an open friendly face and was as fair as a Swede.

Whit, on the other hand, was shorter, of a height with Brick and me. He was as dark as Lanny was light, serious too, and—it was my guess—unleavened by humor.

The newcomers set down their duffel and tossed a copper for bunks. A few tentative questions and answers began to get us acquainted. Little did we know then that we four were to become close friends, sticking together through fair fortune and ill, aye, even unto death, since death was to claim one of us when the time came. Whit took leadership in the half deck, for his was the prestige of having served one year of his apprenticeship in the clipper *Fair Haven*.

"And under Mister Jones, the blasted first mate of the *Flying Cloud*, too," he explained. "May the devil fry him in his own fat!"

A whistle shrilled above our heads.

"That means us!" cried Whit, leaping for the ladder. We tumbled up after him.

On deck men and rigging and boxes and barrels were all mixed up together. There was running and shouting and a confusion of activity that bewildered me. If, in my conceit, I had prided myself that I knew the name and location of every line on the ship, I could not in that moment have picked one from the other. No human being is more helpless than the landsman who takes to sea. Although my interest in

ships dated from earliest childhood, I had never sailed in anything larger than a dory. I found that a ship laid out on the floor of a mold loft is one thing; at sea, something else. We apprentices got in one another's way, fell over the sheets, and were generally useless.

There was a medley of orders half pronounced and unintelligible to our ears. Fortunately a first voyage apprentice is expected to know nothing and we fully lived up to expectation. We could only stand by stupidly or fall on the end of a rope where men were pulling. The wharf was

filled with an excited crowd of spectators. Flags were flying;
bunting lent the dingy dock a festive look. People had come
from all over the city, even from New Jersey and Long
Island, attracted by the fame of the *Flying Cloud*, as well
as by that desire that lies dormant in every human breast,
to see a ship take to the sea.

A brougham drawn by two spanking bays pulled up
with a flourish. From it descended two stylish young ladies
accompanied by their father, Mr. Moses H. Grinnell, the
owner of the *Cloud*. Captain Josiah Perkins Creesy, master
of the ship, appeared, balancing his chronometers; his clear-
ance papers bulging in his pocket. "Perk" Creesy he was,
to his intimates. The Old Man, to us. He was a Marble-
head skipper who had won his reputation in the China tea
trade as master of the *Oneida*. He greeted young Mr. Minturn, who would accompany the pilot as far as Sandy Hook,
and the two men came aboard together through a lane of
admiring bystanders.

The last of the barrels and cases had vanished from the
wharf into the capacious belly of the vessel. She was loaded to
the bolts of her chain plates. The stevedores, pocketing their
wage, laid a course for the nearest saloon. Their work was done.
The *Flying Cloud* could go to the bottom, for all of them!

On the wharf the crowd surged and shouted. A band
was puffing out the strains of "Lost on the Bosom of the
Deep." Funny thing to be playing, thought I with a swallow.
Whit had invested his last dollar in a formidable-looking
accordion, urged upon him by a peddler. Brick Warner
called his farewells to a rosy-cheeked sweetheart. Lanny
laid in a supply of cinnamon balls and a fathom of Irish

Twist tobacco. I had sent ashore three letters for the post: one for Donald McKay, one for my mother, and one for Messina Clarke.

Now we were moving. . . . Cries and cheers and good-bys reached us across a widening gap of water. The *Ajax*, puffing like a porpoise out of water, was nosing the *Cloud* out between the pierheads, lining her up to stem the running tide. We were straining at the capstan bars with:

> Our anchor's a-weigh and our sails they are set,
> Good-by, fare ye well! Good-by, fare ye well!
> And the gals we are leaving we leave with regret,
> Good-by, fare ye well! Good-by!

All the sails had been shaken from their harbor gaskets. A favorable wind was hauling out of the north. Men jumped to set jib and spanker. The yards on the foremast were braced so that the wind would catch the sails aback and thus swing the head off to starboard; while the yards on the main and mizzen were braced in the opposite direction so as to force the ship ahead as soon as her bow canted enough for these sails to draw. There came a hiss of water thrown back from the bows as the *Flying Cloud* heeled to the wind and moved down the river toward Governor's Island and the Lower Bay. Proud she was, like a lady decked out in a new dress, conscious of her beauty and of the admiration she attracted; preening, showing off a bit.

The windows of the buildings along the waterfront were filled with people, waving, shouting, crying, wishing God-speed to us. I stood in the bows by the knightheads, watching Manhattan drop away. A heavy hand was upon me,

for I was leaving the only land I knew, and my people. But the ship was aquiver with life, eager for what lay ahead, and I was aboard her. And feeling this, I knew a sudden lift of the spirit. Ah, it was good to be young, with the world before me!

Ships slipped past, their crews cheering; gulls swooped low at the masthead. The Battery was left behind . . . the hills of Staten Island . . . the desolate line of Coney. . . . The *Flying Cloud* took her first lift to the grounding swells. Beyond the rim of the ocean a new world beckoned.

". . . Winds blow fair for you, *Flying Cloud!* Fine freights swell your hold! Deep harbors wait for you. . . ."

CHAPTER IV

I Make Three Friends—and Get My Sea Legs

UNDER skys'ls, royals, t'gallants, topmast and square lower stun'sls, the *Flying Cloud* fled before a westerly breeze. She was wearing canvas at every point where an earring could be bent, and water boiled white along her lee side. The pilot had been dropped at the Hook, remarking as he swung over the side into his jolly boat that the *Cloud* was as clean a sailer as ever he'd seen. The ship was put on her course. Within two hours the anchors had been catted and fished, gear and tackle set shipshape under the watchful eyes of the mates.

"All hands lay aft!"

The order brought a rush of feet from for'ard. Now the watches were to be chalked, and here it might serve well to give you an idea of the crew that the *Cloud* carried on her maiden voyage. It comprised:

1 Captain	10 boys before	3 stewards
4 Mates	the mast	2 cooks
2 bo'suns	2 carpenters	———
75 able seamen	2 sailmakers	Total, 101 souls

And we were as odd an assortment as ever came out of the Ark, you can believe! Of varying sizes, shapes, and even colors. There were Englishmen among us, Scots, and blue-nose Nova Scotians; "Dutchmen," that term by which Jack means Norwegians, Swedes, Danes, and Germans as well as Hollanders proper. One of the cooks was an African, the other a Fiji Islander, both boasting the complexion of an un-burned coal. Fine men, for the most part; real sailors of the deep-water windships. There was a bond that tied this portion of the crew into obvious kinship: something in the rolling walk, the weather-glancing eye, the horny hands half crooked as if to grasp a rope.

The sea sets her mark upon those who follow her whims, and no mistake. Some of these men had sailed under Perk Creesy on every voyage for five years past; a record of satisfaction in the merchant service and a point which I wish here to stress, for the merchant ships of America have been much blackguarded (principally by other nations) and the treatment of the men by the officers grossly exaggerated.

But there were others among us, dredged from the water-front, scum lured westward in search of gold and easy living. Meager men, these; shifty-eyed and ill found. You will hear more of this portion of the crew later.

A ship's day is divided into equal watches of four hours, except for the watch from 4.00 P.M. to 8.00 P.M., which is split up into two short dogwatches. This device divides equally among the crew the more exacting watches for each forty-eight hours, as you will see if you do a little figuring on your fingers.

The first mate took a piece of chalk and drew a line on the deck from the hatch to the afterhouse. He straightened up and looked us all over with a sharp eye before making his first choice.

"You!" he barked, jerking his thumb toward Nils Olsen, a towering Swede who was limbed like a Viking. Olsen stepped to larboard of the line.

It was the second mate's turn. "All right, you!" He indicated Caleb Winthrop, a Yankee with a seagoing swing to his shoulders. Caleb jumped forthwith to starboard of the line.

Thus the two mates proceeded, making as equal a division of brawn and seamanship among the two watches as might be. We ten apprentices naturally brought up at the last. All of us watched the first mate, whom we had quickly sized up as a "bucko," with dismay in our souls. We quaked inwardly at the prospect of being picked for his watch. One after another we crossed the chalk line. As luck would have it, Brick, Lanny, Whit, and I were chosen by the second mate in due course, and an audible sigh of relief all but escaped us each, I can tell you.

When the watches had been picked, Captain Creesy stepped down from the poop. He walked the length of the chalk line, looking us over. His eyes probed each man's face, weighed the character behind it. He was appraising the muscle and temper of this crew that was to run the *Flying Cloud* to the other end of the world and back. Out of the clew of my eye I observed the Old Man at close range for the first time. A clean-timbered man he was, big in frame and character. He struck awe into the whole ship's company, from first mate to lowliest apprentice. But it was an awe mixed, for the most part, with liking. Besides a mastery of navigation, Captain Creesy had the physical strength to manhandle the toughest of his crew. At the same time he had a courtesy, even gentility of manner, that was called for on clippers that ofttimes numbered gentlewomen among their passengers. Requirements as widely opposed as these bred an extraordinary type of man: overbearing, dictatorial, harsh; polite, genial, gracious. This morning as he stood athwart the chalk line impaling us with his eye, I thought that I had never seen a man more surely bred to walk the quarter-deck. I think so still.

"Well, men," he boomed, in a skys'l-reaching voice, "we are embarked upon a long voyage. Ours is the privilege of sailing the finest ship afloat! We're out to make a record passage for the sake of the owners and our own immortal souls. Now tail onto this: if you do your duty as sailors and obey your officers, you and I will pull together in fine style. If you don't, there'll be hell let loose! If there's any packet rats or sea lawyers aboard, they'd best jump overboard now, before they're heaved. I'll have no sojering aboard my ship. In five minutes the larboard watch goes on duty. The rest of you get into the foc'sle and stow your duffel proper. Now jump!"

He turned abruptly and mounted the lee poop ladder. We stood transfixed for a moment, staring after him, even the old shellbacks impressed in spite of themselves. Those who hadn't sailed with Perk Creesy before knew him by reputation and knew that he was as good as his word.

Some of the men shook their heads wisely as they went forward.

"He's nobody's fool, and that's a fact," observed old Tom Plunkett, one of the two carpenters.

But another man took exception to the statement. "The passage has yet to be run, me hearty," this man remarked with a sneer. "Fool or no, all men is born equal and we's as good as him any week o' Sundays!"

Thus spoke Jeeter Sneed. We all turned to look at him, and didn't like what we saw. Everything about him proclaimed him alien to the sea: eyes that flickered in a dead-white face; loose-lipped mouth twisted into a snarl; a body thin and ill nourished that managed to suggest a certain wiry strength. In Jeeter Sneed we recognized a presence that promised trouble and discord aplenty.

Nils Olsen, the giant with the sea in his eyes, gave vent to an explosive laugh at the man's remark. Looking down from his vast height upon Sneed, he demanded: "So! You vas as good as der Olt Man, yet? Ach! A goot one, dot iss!" We all laughed, and Sneed threw the Scandinavian a black look as he turned away.

There was unanimous dislike of the first mate. We will call him Mister Jones, which name, in view of later developments, will serve better than his own. He was a man whose truculent temper needed but a spark to touch off the explosive; whose authority as second in command was a power to be abused. To his way of thinking, apprentices justified their existence by being the target for his sarcastic humor or the toe of his boot. Brick Warner was the first of us to find this out, and not two minutes after the watch chalking.

"Here you!" Mister Jones bawled at him, "go down to the steward and ask him for the key to the keelson."

Now, the keelson is a technical name for the inner part of a vessel's keel. The key to it, needless to say, is but a jape at the apprentice's expense. Having worked in a ship-builder's office, I knew what a keelson was. Brick, in all probability, did not. Some of the older men were grinning in anticipation of his discomfiture, while Mister Jones was obviously primed for a hearty guffaw. As Brick passed me, I managed a warning wink. His answering flick of the lid showed that he had caught my meaning. With a respectful "Aye, aye, sir" to Mister Jones, he disappeared on his errand.

Reappearing a few minutes later, he touched his cap and said to the first mate, "Beg your pardon, sir, but the steward said he lost the key to the keelson overboard just this morning."

So sly and ingenuous was the manner of his remark, that the men laughed in spite of themselves, while Mister Jones darkened with anger.

"Ye're pretty smart, boy, ain't ye?" he snarled.

"Ye—no, sir," stammered poor Brick.

The mate fetched him a clip alongside the head. Brick hit the deck, blood spurting from his nose. Mister Jones stood over him.

"Maybe that'll take in the slack o' yer jaw tackle," he snapped. "Next time do as you're told, and no chin about it. Anybody else here who's too big fer his breeches?" He looked belligerently around at the circle of us. We could only stare back dumbly, filled with resentment at the injustice of such treatment.

This exhibition gave us fair warning of what to expect from our first mate. Not a rosy prospect, and that's a fact. A ship is a small world: one hundred one men living within a few inches of each other, week after week, month after long month. Grudges take root; the smallest grievances breed hatred. Under the strain of grueling work, bad food, and constant danger, nerves snap and the men are at the mercy of an officer's temper.

To you readers who go down to the sea in books there must inevitably be a certain similarity in deep-water tales. There's always, you complain, the bucko mate, for example, and the hell-driving captain. Well—maybe so. At sea only the tough survive to command. Captains may differ in minor details: one may wear Galways and be a religious fanatic; the other may be clean-shaven and a blaspheming

heathen; yet they're alike, as a porpoise is like a dolphin—different as to species, 'tis true, but of the same genus. At first the harsh discipline, the order enforced at the boot's end, seemed needless and cruel to me.

But I had yet to learn that a ship at sea is a complex fabric, all of whose varying parts must function as a unit; and over that unit a quarter-deck intelligence in control. No longer were we individuals—Enoch Thacher, Brick Warner, Tom Plunkett—we were the muscles and sinews of the ship, flexing in obedience to a higher command. Besides, if the whole truth be told, the owners like a captain who's a driver and a bucko mate to bully the larboard watch!

If Mister Jones subscribed to pattern and quickly earned the hatred of all aboard, our second mate was of different stripe. As easy tempered as a trade wind was Mister Andrews, yet a taskmaster who put up with nothing less than ship-shape work. His great strength commanded the respect of the whole ship's company, as brawn and thew have a way of doing. His arms and chest were tattooed with a collection of sailor's knots, mottoes, and full-rigged ships. When he tensed and relaxed the muscles of his biceps, a native maid danced in jolly fashion. He was seen to bend an iron belaying pin with his two hands, and anyone who had been tempted to impose upon his good nature forthwith changed his mind.

The first duty that he relegated to us of the half deck was care of the livestock! In a pen sheltered by the life-boats lashed atop the for'ard deckhouse, four goats proved themselves the possessors of enviable sea legs. They were blessed as well with stomachs that could digest vegetable fiber, rope yarn, or sea boot. In addition, there were two hogs, ducks, and geese; and hens to furnish omelets for the Old Man's table.

"He must think we shipped to sea to be ruddy farmers!" muttered Brick rebelliously, as he started about his first sea chores with a hoe. "I'd be doing this if I was back home."

"Heave to the life on the ocean wave!" mocked Lanny. "You'll be a sailor yet, m'lad!"

But this particular duty of ours was of short duration, as you will see, and its loss was mourned by none save the Old Man. Brick and Whit and Lanny and I, together with other lubbers of our watch, were already feeling the pangs of seasickness. The increasing pitch of the ship coupled with the breath of our farmyard chores, soon brought things to a crisis. A moment came, when of almost single impulse we bent ourselves over the handiest portion of bulwark. The shellbacks lined up to jape at our discomfort.

"Ther's one sure cure for seasickness, boy," admonished old Tom Plunkett, taking me to one side a few moments later.

"What's that, Tom?" I gasped, feeling as if I had been kicked amidships by a mule.

"Jest drink a quart of warm sea water, and come night you'll be able to eat a jackass and a hamper o' greens!"

A quart of warm sea water . . . the very thought of it was enough to send me back to the bulwark on the run.

"One thing about it," chuckled old Tom to Caleb Winthrop, "he couldn't rightly be said to have a *weak* stomach. He's chuckin' as fur's the rest!"

For three days our wind held, varying only to increase its force. And so multiple were the tasks allotted to every waking minute of our watches, that the time passed in a blur that left no eye for detail. Captain Creesy was testing his ship out, putting her through her paces as a man might a race horse. More and more canvas was being bent at each watch; the resulting stress upon new rigging was observed carefully, each new combination being allowed to show its worth for the length of a watch before another was added. On the third day, with a full gale blowing out of the northwest, we were running under every scrap of storm canvas that even a driver like the Old Man would have dared to set. A constant cry of "All hands!" dragged weary sailors from their watch below to shorten sail that would be made again by the regular watch if the wind slacked up for half an instant. So far the *Flying Cloud* had behaved beautifully under this rugged treatment, surging with a steady rhythm, overtaking each green wave ahead, slicing her way through it and leaping forward to clear herself of the tons of water that mounted astern. She was not a dry ship, however; sometimes her starboard rail was buried for minutes at a time and her decks were awash and swirling.

Still the *Cloud* took her beating and came back for more. How Donald McKay's heart would have swelled with pride could he have seen her! When it seemed that she was carrying as much as she could stand, the Old Man's voice came ringing from the poop:

"Another reef out o' that tops'l and give it to her!"

Then into the shrouds the men sprang and swarmed aloft. Reef points and earrings were cast adrift, the halyards manned, and the released canvas swelled to bursting before the onslaught of the gale. It seemed all that the ship could stagger under, and with the heavy seas bucking the wheel, two men were needed to steer her. Great wings of spume were flung back from the bows, as far aft as the break of the poop. She clipped ahead at a tremendous pace. Still nothing gave way. Preventer braces were rove and hauled taut, tackles were gotten upon the backstays, while the Old Man paced the poop and looked aloft at the drum-tight canvas with a grim smile on his lips. And Mister Andrews chuckled with delight and shouted aloud:

"Bully for you, old tea wagon! You know where you're going!"

The old shellbacks, grouped about the foredeck, speculated on her speed, and shook their heads as they glanced aloft at the straining spars.

Again came the Old Man's voice, "Mister Andrews, out with the topmast stuns'l!"

A gasp escaped the men. Was Perk Creesy plumb daft? Then the mate's order sent them into action, "Lay aloft, you lubbers, and rig out the topmast stuns'l boom!"

The men sprang into the top and the rigging was sent up to them. Tacks and halyards were rove, and the stuns'l boom outrun and lashed fast, while the lower halyards were sent down as a preventer. The sail was bent to the yard and ready for hoisting; the halyards manned. Then

"Way-a-a-ay and up she rises!" as the yard was hoisted fairly up to the block. When the men started to boom-end the sail, the whole ship quivered to her keel. The boom bent like whalebone, and any second we waited to see something carry away. The tough, short spruce bent but did not crack, and with this sail added to her wingspread, the *Flying Cloud* seemed fairly to leap out of the water. The helmsmen fought to hold her within three points of her course, while foam and spray swept aft in stinging deluge.

Aye, the Captain drove her, and no mistake. The shellbacks, bred to a different manner of ship—used to the buoyant cork riding of the East Indiamen—took none too kindly to a vessel that had relatively so little lift to her bows. They grumbled at such treatment, seeing in it a portent of punishment and ill luck ahead.

"The Old Man's carryin' the papers to Davy Jones, sure enough," growled Ben Backstay.

"Aye," croaked Tom Plunkett, "we'll ne'er see the dawn of another payday, and that's sartin. Bendin' on more'n more sail! All three r'yals when we'd orter be under double-reefed t'gansls as 'tis."

"Val," Nils Olsen added his bit, "yust let det Olt Man snap der sticks out uf her yet! Den ve can ship a jury rig dot von't stand sooch treatment. Ve can take it easy den."

But the men who had sailed with Perk Creesy before, and were familiar with his tactics, grunted their derision of the croakers.

"The Old Man orter send for you caulkin' lubbers to tell him how to sail a ship, eh?" they snorted. And the

SAIL-PLAN
of the
CLIPPER

1—flying jib	12—main royal stays'l
2—outer jib	13—mains'l
3—inner jib	14—main tops'l
4—fore topm'st stays'l	15—main t'gallants'l
5—fores'l	16—main royal
6—fore tops'l	17—main skys'l
7—fore t'gallants'l	18—mizzen t'gallant stays'l
8—fore royal	19—mizzen tops'l
9—fore skys'l	20—mizzen t'gallants'l
10—main topm'st stays'l	21—mizzen royal
11—main t'gallant stays'l	22—mizzen skys'l

23—spanker

grumbling ceased for the time being under the lash of their scorn.

But if the Old Man was driving us all remorselessly, he spared himself no less. Since leaving port, he had been on the quarter-deck night and day. He cat napped in a chair lashed by the binnacle and leaped to his feet with an oath if the ship fell off so much as half a point.

As darkness shut in on the night of July 11, I was aroused by a banging on the scuttle and the ringing cry, "All hands! Save ship!" In half deck and foc'sle we were to become used to that summons erelong, but hearing it that wild night for the first time it brought me to my feet at a bound. Brick fell out of his bunk and landed on all fours, with Whit and Lanny tumbling after him. I have no recollection of reaching deck. Suddenly I was there, waist-deep in swirling water.

What a sight greeted my eyes! The blackness of the night pressed down upon me like a hand. Clouds raced at the masthead. Beyond the bulwarks, mountains moved in wild flight, pale on the crests where the gale tore off foam and flung it into the valleys. The wind whistled through the straining rigging. A terrible sight to a landlubber. It was like the end of a world.

I fought to keep my balance on the plunging deck. Men pushed past me. Voices came out of the welter, fragments of speech borne off on the wind. As I rounded a corner of the house, a sea sheeted over the weather bulwark and caught me in its rush—flung me like a chip into the lee scuppers. The sea swept aft. Pigsty, hencoop, ducks, and goats disappeared in the blink of an eye.

"Enjoy your swim?"

A hand gripped the collar of my jacket and jerked me to my feet. Mister Andrews bulked above me. He was dressed in oilskins and sea boots. I realized that if ever I would need mine, it would be tonight. Too late now. I'd know better next time. I could dimly make out the Old Man on the poop beside the straining wheelsmen. The first mate was in his place on the foc'sle head. I fought my way at the second mate's heels into the waist. Men were clearing the ropes for action. They manned the clew garnets and buntlines that were to snug the sail up to the yard. It seemed to me that no human power could take that sail in. It leaped and fought with the strength of ten lions; it slatted and bellowed. Chain sheets banged. Idiotic it seemed to be pulling here on these ropes—man pitting his puny strength against the storm's might. But haul we did, with every atom of strength. Beef, sinew, muscle, and guts; we gave it all to the job. Slowly the battle was being won, bit by bit, inch by inch. At last the fighting sail was dragged close up to the yard. Then it was:

"Aloft and furl!"

I admit to a feeling of relief that the apprentices were considered still too green to be allowed to lay aloft in a storm. It seemed impossible that any man could climb that wildly swaying rigging, crawl out onto a plunging yard, and beat a sail into submission, all in blackness so dense that you could scarce see two yards ahead.

Then above the whine of the wind, an ominous sound came to our ears, a sound like the groan of a giant wracked by supernatural pain. Looking upward, I saw against the

surface of the mainmast, not ten feet above deck, a widening crack as broad as my hand was long.

The mainmast had sprung.

Orders were hurled out of the darkness. Sheets were loosed on the run. The freed canvas billowed and banged. But the ship responded, righted herself as the men strained at the clew lines, made them fast, then swarmed aloft to try to secure the booming canvas. There came another groan from the spar as the crack widened—agonizing to hear. Those masts of hard pine, doweled together, bolted and hooped over all with iron—strong enough to withstand anything, you would have said, and yet. . . . I looked aloft at the men clinging to the mainyard supported by that weakening spar and knew a thrill of utter fear; fear for them, for all of us; for the *Flying Cloud*.

The Old Man was bellowing orders to cut the weather sheet. That done, and the strain on the mast released, the ominous crack began to close up. Those of us on deck were set to fishing the mainmast with spars lashed to the starboard side, while the men aloft sent down royal and t'gallant yards, and took stuns'l booms off lower and tops'l yards to relieve the weakened mast.

It was daylight before my watch tumbled below. I was so altogether weary with the labor and the excitement of the night that I could scarce stagger. Passing Chips, he demanded:

"Well, me b'y, an' what do ye think o' life on the ocean wave now?"

"It's—it's all right," I managed, "but do—do you get many of these hurricanes?"

Chips threw back his head and laughed uproariously. "Hurricanes, eh? Shiver me timbers, this is naught but a proper blow! *Hurricanes*, he says! Ho! Ho!"

Naught but a proper blow? What would it be like off Cape Horn then? Surely Chips was pulling my leg.

I look back now and smile at my very greenness. It *was* naught but a proper blow. Chips was not pulling my leg.

CHAPTER V

MY FIRST FIGHT—AND AN ENEMY MADE

IN OUR half-deck cabin all was confusion. My sea chest was sloshing back and forth across the floor, its contents half spilled out and slopping about with those of the other three occupants. Pannikins, sea boots, duffel and gear— what a jumble it was! Brick and I had recovered from our attack of seasickness while Whit, with his greater experience of windships, had known scarcely a twinge. But Lanny was laid out in his bunk, the only sign of life from him being a low groan now and again. He had small interest in the chaos of the half deck, or in anything else for that matter, unless it might have been *terra firma*.

"One good thing about that blow last night," observed Whit, wringing out his reefer before putting it on, "no more farmyard chores for us! Lord lumme! When that wave hit us, there wan't so much as a hog's bristle or bent nail to show where the Old Man's pigsty had been!"

Brick felt his jaw with rueful fingers. It was still swollen from his early encounter with Mister Jones. "Too bad the first mate couldn't 'a been in the pigsty instead o' that pig," he observed. "That's where he belongs anyhow."

Whit grinned. "Didn't I warn you that bucko was a tough 'un? You'd orter had more sense than try to be smart with him. Didn't I serve under him for a year in the *Fair Haven*, in his watch, too? 'Whittlesy,' said he to me at the end of the voyage, 'I've been to sea, man and boy for thirty year, but you're the *wust* sailor ever I see! You'd orter shipped on a whaler,' says he, 'ther's enough o' the bone in yer head!' That's why he didn't pick me for his watch again this trip, I cal'late." Whit drew the reefer over his head and sat down on the edge of his bunk to struggle with his shoes. Shoes, feet, and socks were still wet and it made hard going.

"There was luck to that," said I.

"Aye, and that's a fact."

"Better get up on your pins, Lanny," advised Brick, "or the bucko'll be down here and haul you out by the scruff o' the neck."

The only response from the bunk was a low groan.

"Chips knows a good cure for seasickness," I suggested. "A quart of warm sea water, now——"

The groan came louder from the bunk this time and I desisted for the common good. It was astonishing, I thought,

as I dipped my raw hands into a pail of hot beef pickle, the number of cuts and bruises that we of the half deck had picked up in our few short days at sea. The unexpected plunges of the ship, for which nothing in our lives ashore had prepared us, hurled us continually against jutting angles of wood and iron. Already our hands were puffed and bleeding with unaccustomed hauling on wet ropes. New sets of muscles whose existence we had never dreamed of made themselves known, each with a separate ache. But greatest hardship of all—we could not get enough sleep! Four hours on and four off, theoretically. But our skipper was a driver out to make a record passage around the Horn. As a rule, no sooner had we closed our eyes when a mighty clatter set up on the scuttle and a voice roared:

"All ha-ands! Shorten sail!"

That order meant business. We soon learned that if it was just "all hands" you could take a reasonable amount of time to it. But "shorten sail" meant that you must reach the deck at one bound or take the consequences and the rope's end. The orders themselves were couched in a language that might well have been Fijian, for aught we could gather of its meaning. For example, at the command, "All hands shorten and furl sail," we apprentices could only stand by stupidly as the older men manned clew ropes, buntlines, leech lines, downhauls and brails, having the bunt ropes and jiggers overhauled and ready for hooking to the gluts; and hands ready by the halyards, outhauls, and bowlines, to let them go.

"Aloft, topmen!" came the mate's second command.

He allowed the men time to reach the futtock rigging.

Then, "Aloft, lower yard men!"

Then it all came fast and furious: "Haul taut! Clew up! Haul down—lie out and furl! Gather up that slack proper and pass the leeches. Skin that sail smooth in the headband! You in the blue shirt, keep that bunt square in the slings or I'll knock seven bells out o' you!"

"Lie in, down booms, and down from aloft!"

Small wonder that we first voyagers could only stand with mouth agape at such a bewildering performance. We were still too green to be allowed aloft and I looked forward with dread to the moment when the order "aloft and furl!" should be directed at me. How would I fare, two hundred feet above a plunging deck, trying to fist sail in the teeth of a gale? Resolutely I forced the prospect out of my mind. Sooner or later it would come, that moment, but until then——

The bell that struck in our watch sounded on the wheelhouse, and the foc'sle bell took up the echo. Brick and Whit and I tumbled up on deck, leaving Lanny groaning in his bunk below. Smoke issued from the funnel of the galley and we filed for'ard with pannikins in hand. Hunger by now was gnawing at our healthy young vitals and we needed no encouragement to break our fast.

The galley of the *Flying Cloud* was placed well for'ard. Here within a wooden box some twelve feet square, the two cooks carried on their endless work. The African and the Fijian were each known impartially as "Doctor." An opening in the side of the galley looked out on the main deck. Through it we could see the Fijian stirring furiously among his pots and pans while the African's black face framed itself in white bulkhead as we filed past. To each of us he ladled out our rations.

Speculation ran high as to what it was we ate. Only the cooks and the Almighty knew the terrible secret. It passed by the name of *lobscouse*, and if you ask me what was in it, to this day I can only hazard a guess. Pilot bread pounded to bits, perhaps; a hunk of "salt horse," a scrap of pork, a moldy potato or two, all stewed up together with this and that. The sea puts up with no coddling of her men and we were to be held strictly to our "pound and pint." The Spaniards, who boast a knack with proverbs, have one to the effect that hunger makes the best sauce. An apt observation, since before long we relished our *'scouse* with the keen edge of a sea appetite and cleaned up our pannikins till they shone in the sun like a bald man's pate.

The deep-water men accepted this fare naturally, as they accepted everything else at sea. Not for them the eggs from the Old Man's table or the pies or the soft bread. They were foc'sle hands and they knew their fare. But Jeeter Sneed and others of his stripe, who had been raising their voices in complaint of one thing or another ever since leaving port, early seized upon the food as a cause for special grievance.

"Look at this dish o' bilge!" commented Sneed in a loud voice, holding up his pannikin for all to see. "Swill fit fer hogs, that's what it is! It's a blinkin' outrage to offer it to *men!*"

He rose to his feet and crossed to the weather bulwark where I was finishing the remainder of my *'scouse*. I had made no effort to hide my opinion of the man and he knew it. As he drew directly abeam of me, he emptied his pan to wind'ard. The wind caught the "bilge" and flung it back in my face.

"Did you do that on purpose?" I shouted, seeing red.

"Suppose I did—what then?"

The man's twisted sneer blurred before my eyes. I cracked him across the face with all the strength I could muster.

Sneed drew in his breath like the hiss of a snake. "You ——!" he cursed, and reached for his sheath knife.

"Here! Here!" roared Mister Andrews, coming around a corner of the house. "If there's any fightin' aboard this ship, it's goin' to be fair and square. Bare fists and naught else. Up on the foc'sle head, you two, and the best man wins!"

I was in for it. I looked at Sneed's rangy height and realized that I was going to get a good drubbing. Well, maybe I could get in a few good ones on the packet rat before he laid me out. As we marched toward the foc'sle, surrounded by all the free men of the watch, Brick and Whit took me each by an arm and whispered advice in my hot ears.

"He's got a foot more reach than you," cautioned Brick, "so keep in close and don't give him a chance to swing."

"Aye, that's the part o' wisdom," Whit amended, "keep in close and catch him with a right hook to the jaw. Then follow it up with a left uppercut before he can say Hunky Dory. That'll take the wind out of his mains'l!"

Keep in close . . . right hook to the jaw . . . then a left uppercut! Sounded easy, when you said it like that. Of course Sneed wouldn't have any ideas of his own—just going to stand there like a bollard post and let me whang at him!

"I'll ship what's left home to your mother," grinned Whit, giving me a dig in the ribs.

"Too bad," Brick chuckled, "they didn't give you time to make your will. I'd speak up for that spyglass of yours!"

"Oh, stow it!" I answered testily.

The men formed a circle on the foc'sle head. The ship was sailing full and by; no call to touch sheet or halyard. Here was a pleasant diversion for a man to while away a watch.

"Come on, b'ys! Ready for action!" bellowed Mister Andrews. "And don't fergit I'm here to see ther's fair play. Any dirty work out of you and you'll know the end o' my boot!"

I stripped off my shirt and tightened up my belt the way I had seen professional fighters do, mustering up the while such show of confidence as I was able.

"Remember what I told you," cautioned Brick.

"At it, b'ys!"

"Eat 'im up, Jeet!"

Sneed had pulled off his shirt and I saw the muscles stretched like wires over his lean carcass. I squared off and stuck out my chin at a bellicose angle. For a second I thought I saw a flick of fear in Sneed's eyes.

"Afraid?" I jeered.

"I'm going to kill you!" came his answer.

Perhaps it was the conviction behind the words that sent me forward at a bound. Keep in close . . . right hook. . . . I closed my eyes and swung with all my might. My fist connected with a crack and jarred my arm to the shoulder. Left uppercut. . . . My left drove viciously and my knuckles buckled under the blow.

There was a thud and a groan. I opened astonished eyes. I expected at any moment to be annihilated. There was Sneed—face down on the deck!

"Get back!" yelled the mate at me. "You've done enough!"

I went cold. Had I killed the man? What a beginning to my life at sea! I heard voices shouting excitedly: "Up and at him, Jeet!" "Lay into him, Thach!" And from the mate: "A bucket of water there. Tail onto it!"

My heart was in my mouth as Mister Andrews dashed water into Sneed's face. Would he never open his eyes? . . . He blinked for a moment, as if he couldn't believe his senses, then he looked at me. I felt my blood chill before the malevolence of his eyes.

"Thacher wins, fair and proper!" cried the mate. "Up on yer pins, Sneed, and shake hands!"

"I'll see him rot fust!" snarled Sneed. He moved close up to me, and as long as I live I will remember the concentrated venom behind his words.

"I'll square this up with you, Thacher, if I die for it," he said.

"Come, come," interposed the mate. "That's no way for a man to lose a fight."

But Sneed slunk off with his crony Slim Harkins and disappeared in the gloom of the foc'sle. As I made my way back into the waist, Brick and Whit cracked me on the back.

"See what my good advice did for you?" gloated Brick. "It was that uppercut that finished him off, the scum!"

"Gee Whittaker, whyn't you tell us you had a punch like a mule's left leg?" Whit demanded.

Caleb Winthrop joined us and tapped me on the arm. "Take my advice and keep to wind'ard o' that sea lawyer from now on," he warned. "He's a bad 'un and no mistake."

"Aye," assented Tom Plunkett, " 'tis lucky fer you the Old Man had the mates grind the point off every man's sheath knife or you'd be slit from clew to earring afore morning!"

It didn't need these gloomy forebodings to assure me that I had made an enemy. I had whipped Jeeter Sneed in front of the whole watch. "I'll square this up with you, Thacher, if I die for it!" he had said. Young as I was, I knew that those words were not idly spoken. He would make good his threat if ever I gave him the opportunity, alow or aloft.

Well—I would follow Caleb Winthrop's advice and keep to wind'ard of the man wherever possible. It wouldn't be an easy feat within the narrow space of a ship. But there was a new confidence running like fire through my veins, a consciousness of discovered strength. The sweat of victory salted my lips and I relished its taste.

I had won my fight.

With the wind still holding half a gale, the *Flying Cloud* fled due southeast. Now that the Old Man had tested her out and sprung her mainmast doing it, he drove her less brutally of necessity. We of the half deck and foc'sle felt the release from strain in a more regular resumption of our watches. Turning out on deck with Brick Warner the

morning after my fight with Jeeter Sneed, Mister Andrews' voice hailed us:

"Lay aloft, you lubbers, and furl them r'yals!"

The dreaded moment had come. Involuntarily we paused.

"Tail onto it, you sojers!"

Brick scrambled into the fore shrouds; I into the main.

"Here! Don't hold onto them ratlines! It's the shrouds you wants, me b'ys." Mister Andrews stood there with his arms folded across his broad chest, grinning mightily. "And no lookin' down, remember!"

Cautiously I made my way upward, my cold hands clutching the shrouds with a beginner's grip. I didn't know then that men who fell from the rigging were usually old hands grown careless. Looking neither to right nor left, up I climbed until I was stopped by the futtock shrouds at the head of the lower rigging. The ship was heeling at such an angle that it seemed as if the wind itself helped speed me up the narrowing path of ratlines. The futtock shrouds stretch outward to the maintop. To negotiate them, you have to turn on your back and, with your feet toward the mast and your head out in space, haul yourself up by sheer muscle.

Out over these futtocks I pulled myself, scarce daring to breathe.

"Go on!" bellowed the mate.

I reached for a hold in the topmast rigging. Step by step I climbed, up a conglomeration of ropes that seemed to have no end. How different they had looked drawn on paper in Donald McKay's drafting room! As far up as I could see, they stretched, like the web of a mammoth spider, and

seemingly no more secure for a man to trust his life to. My legs felt jerky, my arms nerveless. I was sick and dizzy as I paused at the topmast head.

"This is crazy," I argued with myself. "The royal— can't furl it if I *do* reach it. . . . Look at Brick! How'd he ever get up there?"

Ahead of me on the foremast, halfway up to the crosstrees, was Brick.

"Up with you, Thacher!" came the mate's inexorable voice from below.

I looked upward at the maze of ropes leading to the haven of the crosstrees. What an endless stretch of them between me and the platform, I thought, as I climbed. The crosstrees—more difficult to surmount than the futtocks had been. I looked longingly at the "lubber's hole" and wished that I had the courage to try to sneak through it. But I still retained sense enough to know that should I try it, I'd catch fire and brimstone when I regained deck. With many a misgiving, I laid hold of the crosstree ropes and pulled myself up—up to the wooden platform. A cry of relief broke from me and I sank down on my knees. *That* was over.

"Keep going there!" yelled the mate from below, his voice pitched to carry across the widening distance.

By now my brain was empty of every thought but my insecurity and the terrible fear of plunging to the deck. But there was no defying that inexorable voice. Growl you may but go you must, says the sailor; and it's a fact. Gingerly I picked my way up to the t'gallant rigging. Not so long a climb as the topmast. It came to an end at the t'gallant masthead. I laid hold of the t'gallant yard and planted both my feet in the footrope swinging from its stirrups beneath. There I clung for dear life. The skys'l yard had been struck, and nothing remained above my head but the bare pole of the royal mast crossed by the royal yard. For the first time I dared a furtive glance downward. The blood froze in my veins.

What must it be like up here in a gale, clinging to this yard with one hand and fisting sail with the other? I shuddered at the thought of it. The mate's voice, diminished by distance, broke in on my speculations:

"Go on! Up with you, you blasted sojer!"

For a moment I paused, torn between the necessity for going up or the impulse to return to deck and take the consequences. I looked up at the royal mast. If I failed, I should never have to face Messina Clarke or anyone else again, for I should be dead. With one hand I reached out and caught the royal backstay, swinging my feet free of the ratlines. There was a split second when I hung by a single hand, before my numb legs could twist themselves round the backstay; a sheer drop of two hundred feet. Then I was astride the royal yard!

As soon as I caught my breath, I was mightily proud of myself. I looked up at the remaining feet of bare pole surmounted by the ball of the main-truck that was the last thing between me and the sky, and shouted:

"By the Great Horn Spoon, Cap'n Clarke! I did it!"

Now I dared to look around me. Forgetting the pull of gravity, dizziness had disappeared. Nothing overhead but a sky swept with mares' tails. Below, the sharp-edged

horizon forming a perfect circle. Under my feet an acre of canvas drum-tight in the breeze. And there was I, riding through space on the great arc cut by the masthead, the sun washing with gold the white-curving sails. To be there was to be as close to heaven as a man has any right to demand in this world. In front of me, on eye's level, rose the spire of the foremast. I saw Brick Warner then, clinging to the royal yard. We shouted to each other and waved with one hand free.

"Ahoy, up there!" came the mate's voice. "Furl that r'yal and brisk about it!"

Cautiously I lay out on the yard, my feet fumbling for the footrope. I cast adrift the gaskets. The sail whipped away from me and thrashed like a banner. A pretty pickle, I thought—that square of heaviest cotton duck, slatting and banging above my head. One glancing blow from it, and I would be flung like a crumb from a carpet into the sea below. The motion of the ship, slight enough on deck, was magnified at this great height and the royal yard was cutting capers across the sky. At first I dared do nothing but hang on for life and limb.

"Tail onto it up there!"

I picked up the bunt and lay to it. Clutching the canvas as best I could, I dragged it in slowly, bit by bit. After many luckless attempts, I was able to lay hold of the gasket. Then I pulled it as tight as I could and made it fast.

Gingerly I crawled on my belly out to the weather yard-arm. The banging sail was like to knock me spinning. Somehow, holding to the jackstay with desperate grip, I clutched the sail with my free hand and began the struggle.

Time and again it whipped itself out of my grasp just as I
had begun to make it fast to the yard. I felt a jab of pain
as the nail ripped off my index finger. My muscles ached
with the strain. Each time the sail tore itself free the
whole heartrending business had to be gone through with
again. At last, when I felt plumb tuckered, I succeeded in
getting the gaskets passed and the sail lashed to the yard.
The leeward side gave me less trouble. At last the sail
was snugged fast. It has taken me the best part of an
hour.

I climbed into the rigging, noting out of the clew of my
eye that Brick was still fighting the windward gaskets of his
sail. I reached the t'gallant rigging when a voice hailed me.
The mate's.

"D'you call that a shipshape job?" he shouted.

"Yes!" I yelled back.

"WHAT?"

"Yes—sir," I amended.

"Then lay out there and make a better job of it, or by
the Powers, I'll have you keelhauled!"

There was nothing to do but climb aloft, hand over
weary hand, and cast loose once more those hard-fought
gaskets. I let them go as reluctantly as if they'd been my
hold on life. The freed sail ballooned out over my head and
there was the whole heartbreaking job to be gone through
with again. Determinedly I tackled it, dragging in the canvas inch by inch. Once again the gaskets passed, a little
brisker this time. Finally all was snug. I figured that I
had clipped a good ten minutes off the first trial. Once
more I swung into the rigging for the descent.

"Lay out on that yard, you bloody sojer, and furl that r'yal proper!"

Aye, growl you may but go you must. Swallowing my wrath as best I might, I lay out on that accursed yard and once more cast loose the sail. Bit by bit I fought to take it in again; then with the uttermost care I skinned down every bulge in the canvas as tight as my aching muscles could pull. And I was forced to admit that this was a neater job than my two previous attempts. But I doubted that I had clipped any time from the operation. My arms and legs felt like lead. When I swung into the rigging for the descent, my fingers were nerveless and I sank down thankfully on the platform of the crosstrees.

"Cast adrift that r'yal!" bellowed the mate furiously, "or come down here and take the rope's end!"

For one wild moment I thought of accepting his invitation. No punishment could have been worse than this. My hands were covered with blood and every muscle of my body twitched with a separate ache. The man's an inhuman monster, I thought.

". . . I hope he ends in a shark's belly, or dies of scurvy, or . . ."

With a sensation of utter despair, I climbed out on that royal yard and cast loose the sail once more.

After four hours of it, I was permitted to slide down to deck. It was my watch below and I fell into my bunk more dead than alive. Body and brain alike were numb. A hard school, you may say. Aye, that it is. But stowing a royal was something I was able to pride myself on forever after.

Rousing out of my stupor shortly, I called out to Whit in the bunk below, "Where's Brick?"

"Last I saw of him he was fistin' the fore r'yal. Hasn't come down yet," was his answer.

I fell into an exhausted slumber, dreaming that I was stowing sail on a mighty yard supported by no mast! And every time I jammed my fist into the billowing canvas, the canvas turned into a leering face, while Jeeter Sneed's voice mocked:

"I'll square this up with you, Thacher, if I die for it!"

CHAPTER VI

A Passport from Neptune—and Trouble in the Foc'sle

THE *Flying Cloud* had picked up the northeast trades. With this rousing breeze on her starboard quarter and every sail set from spanker to flying jib and drawing handsomely, she was laying knots behind her. Here, for 20 degrees of ocean, the wind hauls out of the east-northeast and blows scarcely shifting a hand's breadth the year round. All hands had been sent aloft to set the stuns'ls, which added some fifteen feet to the ship's wingspread. With the yards braced up just clear of the backstays, we fled south beneath a summer sky.

There was no need now to touch sheet or stay, and for that we greenhorns were grateful, for we had been serving an unrelenting apprenticeship under the watchful eyes of the mates: day and night loosing and setting sail, clewing up canvas and furling it, reefing tops'ls and courses, shaking out reefs, and mastheading the tops'ls to the rolling rhythm of the chanteys.

Flying fish weather, the oldsters were calling it, and the reason was not far to seek: flying fish fled in skimming shoals at our approach, the sun glinting on their glassy wings. Dolphins played about our bows, arching, leaping, diving in their sportive capers. Beautifully formed fish they were, whose glistening bodies threw back rainbow colors from sun and sky and sea.

The days now were a sheer delight. Running down the trades in a windship is to savor sea life at its finest: the incomparable blue of tropic water, shot through with arrows of dancing light; sea birds white against the sky, motionless save for the quick inquiring turn of their heads; the untroubled rim of the horizon, sharp as the edge of a sword where it cleaves the lighter blue of sky. . . . You who spend your lives in the pallid north can have but small idea of this rich warmth! Go and see it!

There was work to be done aplenty, for a ship—like a watch—is always out of repair, and it is part of a mate's duty to see that no man is ever idle. But our watches on deck were no longer spent waist-deep in swirling water, struggling with stubborn ropes and blocks. Grand fun it was to be aloft on some gently swaying yard, two hundred feet above ship and ocean, glancing down occasionally at the wake stretching white and straight as far as eye could see, telling its story of a fine passage in the making. And birds darting low to look at you, their eyes bright with curiosity, their hoarse voices falling not unpleasantly on the ear. Aye, don't read about it! Go and see it for yourselves!

Our heavier clothing had been put aside till it should be needed again in the sterner latitudes to the south. We were reduced to duck pants with or without undershirt, and our bare feet rejoiced in their deliverance from sodden boots and shoes. But the best interests of veracity compel the admission that this tropic weather was not an undiluted blessing— for out of every crack and crevice in the ship cockroaches swarmed. Hundreds, thousands, finally millions of them. You would have said that a new ship like the *Cloud* would

have been free of such pests. No sir-ee! Though we killed
them by the thousand, fresh battalions filled the places
of the slain. They seemed to materialize out of the air
itself. They devoured every crumb left in the locker. They
were sturdy swimmers and rode like corks on the surface of
every mug of coffee from the galley. Eventually we acknowledged ourselves whipped and turned into our bunks at night
with our shoes on to keep them from gnawing the soles of
our feet!

Now in the trades we apprentices began to learn something of the "Whole business of being a seaman," as our
Indentures put it. On quiet nights there were hours of study.
Under Mister Andrews' indulgent eye, we worked up the
noon sights by way of practice and learned to write entries
for the log. There were two logs kept on shipboard: the
Official Log of the Old Man, wherein were entered details
of hazard at sea, injury, death, trouble with the crew, etc.;
and the Navigation Log kept by the first mate, whose
entries concerned winds, course, speed and barometer read-
ings. It was this latter log that we must learn to write up.
At night, with the ship running easily, we searched to find
all the stars of first magnitude and to distinguish one from
another.

Bowditch's Navigator was Mister Andrews' Bible. He
fairly crowed over any necessities of storm by day that enabled
him to display his skill at double altitudes of the fixed stars
by night. And when for a span of days and nights there
had been no help possible for sun, moon, or stars, his dead
reckoning was faultless. He could have navigated a ship,
I truly believe, by the movements of the upper and lower

clouds, the behavior of the birds, and the wind against his cheek. A handful of degrees was less accurate it seemed than that sixth sense which had its roots in his vast practical knowledge.

Sometimes in the dining saloon, by the light of the gently swaying lamp, we spread our books about us and belabored our brains with the knotty problems of navigation and logarithms and rules of the road. Ah, it was all fun, you can believe! The Roaring Forties and Cape Horn—they lay ahead, grim with threat as the oldsters never ceased to remind us. But we were filled with the spirit of adventure and so, sufficient unto the day . . .

* * * * * * * *

On our twenty-first day out we knew that we were in the region of the Equator, and we of the half deck were speculating as to the ceremonies of Crossing the Line, fearsome tales of which we had all heard.

It happened to be my trick at the wheel that morning from ten till twelve o'clock. As the sun drew near the meridian, the Old Man and the first mate were occupied, as usual, in taking independent sights. After Captain Creesy had worked the observation, he turned to the mate, and I thought I caught an unaccustomed glint of humor in his eye.

"Mister," he observed, "we're just abaft the Line. Send a man aloft to report if anything's in sight."

"Aye, aye, sir," responded the mate solemnly. And shortly thereafter a voice sang out from the fore t'gallant masthead:

"Sail Ho-o-!"

"Where away?" cried the Old Man.

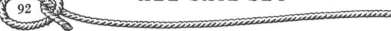

"Dead ahead, sir. Bearing straight down on us!"

"What manner of ship is she?"

"I—can't rightly say, sir. Might be pirates!"

"Turn all hands to!" the Old Man shouted, busy with his spyglass.

When the apprentices of the other watch appeared, we were all dispatched to the 'tweendecks to break open a case of firearms. But no sooner were we safely below decks, than the scuttle was banged shut above our heads and there we were, trapped as snug as a parcel of rats.

Now we heard a great commotion on deck and a rush of feet above our heads. Then a deep voice seemed to boom forth from beneath our bows:

"*Flying Cloud*—aho-o-y-!"

The Old Man answering: "Ho-o-! Halloo-o-!"

"Got any landlubbers aboard?"

"Aye, aye, Neptune!"

"I'm right glad to hear it," boomed the voice (which put us in mind somewhat of Tom Plunkett's). "How many?"

"Oh, ten or a dozen likely lads who are willing to lose their beards if they can get a passport."

"Back your main yards," replied Father Neptune, "and I'll come aboard and trim their beards in two shakes of a gull's rudder!"

There was a scrambling in the chains and a thudding of feet on deck as the Captain welcomed his guests with loud commotion.

"Come, come," cried Father Neptune impatiently, "bring 'em forth! I've several ships to visit before nightfall. Barber, whet up that razor! We'll give these lads a passport to navigate these waters for the rest o' their natural lives— if they don't die a natural death afore that."

As luck would have it, when the mate opened the scuttle, I was the one nearest to hand, and he grabbed me by the scruff and hauled me up on deck. There I stood blinking in the strong sunlight. Father Neptune was awaiting me, surrounded by his court and flanked by Mrs. Neptune. His Majesty sported a beard of frayed hemp while his rope-yarn locks were crowned with a coronet of gulfweed. His hand clutched a harpoon in lieu of a scepter. Mrs. Neptune, whose cheeks bloomed with a flush of red lead, was clothed in a gown of sailcloth with a fish-net veil. When she smiled, her four missing front teeth proclaimed her kinship to Caleb Winthrop.

"Ye're a likely-looking lad," said His Majesty, addressing himself to me. "I want subjects like you. But there are certain purification rites which must be performed before you will be worthy to enter my domain. First, you must be shaved. Barber, apply the brush and hand me my razor!"

Zeke Rilling was the "barber" and he laid about my chin and lower jaw with a huge brush that had been dipped in tar and fish oil.

"Have you ever been shaved before, young fellow, m'lad?" asked Father Neptune.

"No," I replied respectfully.

"What say?" he demanded.

"No, sir!" I answered yet again.

"Louder, please!" cried His Majesty. "My hearing ain't so good."

Whereupon I opened my mouth and shouted, "No-o-o-!"

Scarce had I opened my mouth when the barber plunged the tar brush down my throat and I sputtered and gagged to the vast delight of the audience.

"Has my razor a proper edge to it, Barber?" asked Neptune.

"Aye, aye, sir. Keen as a shark's tooth you'll find it," came the answer.

The "razor" was fashioned from an old iron hoop and had an edge like a bucksaw. Father Neptune manipulated it in much the same manner, and every time it was drawn across my jaws it left a wake of blood. Involuntarily I opened my mouth to protest, which afforded the barber another chance to thrust with his tar brush.

"Now speak right up, lad," said Father Neptune, when this ordeal had come to an end. "There is a pledge you must swear to if you want to be one of my subjects. Do you swear never to eat meat when you can get fish; that is, unless you prefer meat?"

"I do," I answered, keeping my lips as tightly closed as possible.

"Talk louder, m'lad. There's a fog in my ears. Do you swear never to swim when you can walk; that is, unless you prefer to swim?"

"Yes!" I muttered between clenched teeth.

"Come, come! I can't hear you!" protested Father Neptune. "Hand the lad my speaking horn so's he can make himself heard. Do you swear never to drink grog when you can drink water; that is, unless you prefer grog? Speak out!"

I put the horn to my lips and opened my mouth to shout, "I do!" when the barber emptied a bucket of bilge down the horn. I flung the accursed thing aside, but not before I had been compelled to swallow a goodly bit to save myself from suffocating. As I gagged and sputtered, Neptune bellowed:

"Give the lad his passport!"

At this same moment the plank on which I was seated was knocked from under me and I found myself sprawling feet over ears in the water. For one wild second I thought that they had thrown me overboard. I struck out, to save myself, and barked my shins against planking. To my sheepish amazement I found that I was wallowing about in the ship's longboat which had been filled and placed strategically for the purpose. Soaked to the skin, I scrambled out to the japes and horselaughs of the side lines.

Now that I was an initiate, I could take my place in the audience and raise my voice at the plight of my shipmates as, one by one, they were led before Father Neptune. They were all shaved in succession, and the proceedings varied somewhat with each one, thus providing a continuous source of laughter for the jolly sons of Neptune.

The ceremonies, I knew, varied on each ship according to the temper of the commander and the good nature of the crew. Usually they were no more than harmless horseplay, but I had heard of instances where the joke had been carried to such lengths as to border on tragedy. In point of fact, many sailors of the '50's had such a dread of the mysterious ceremonies which were supposed to take place at the Crossing

of the Line that nothing could induce them to sign on a ship bound south of the Equator.

*   *   *   *   *   *   *   *

There is a region just above and below the Lazy Line that is known to charts and skippers as "the area of calms and variables." More commonly, the doldrums—a baffling belt of weather where winds and currents follow no known laws, and the temper of a ship's crew is strained to snapping point.

For some days before we entered this region the northeast trades had slackened, then finally disappeared. With them vanished the sparkling sea. The skies were sultry with thunderheads and fretted with flares of heat lightning, while the masts of the *Flying Cloud* seemed almost to scrape at the low-lying clouds. A glassy calm flattened the surface of the sea and in the distance a vortex on the horizon lifted in a coppery spout of moving water. The doldrums—they held us prisoned in their grip. Cats-paws of fickle wind stirred up out of nowhere to keep us busy, for not a breath must we lose. We were forever hauling round the yards to take advantage of each shifting breeze.

The sails slatted and jeered at us in the fickle airs, airs that at any moment might become a dangerous threat to a ship wearing full canvas. Lightning lit up the surrounding ocean to ghastly brilliance. The ear-splitting crashes that followed bespoke its nearness. Between the crashes, the stillness was so profound that the ear buzzed with the silence. Our sails sagged, inert, dejected. Then rain descended, a stinging deluge, a vertical curtain of water that struck the decks with a loud drumming and splashed upward in spitting cataracts.

We stopped up the scuppers to let the decks fill with the fresh water, then brought out every available bucket and pan. We took off our clothes and found long-forgotten bits of soap and knew the luxury of sweet water against our skins. We remembered laundry, and soon shirts and pants and drawers were hanging from every stay, like a wash-day harbor decoration. Still the deluge descended. Water oozed from every pore of the ship while the ropes swelled in the throats of the blocks and became unmanageable. Grueling work they made for hands grown soft with soaking.

The area of calms and variables. . . . At one moment the *Cloud* lay lifeless, without a quiver on the plane of the sea. Again, under the drive of a sudden-bursting squall, she would be bowling along with her lee rail buried, and an anxious mate watching for the moment when she could take no more. Then it was:

"All hands to shorten sail!"

And a merry time we had of it, you can believe.

The sullen tempers in the foc'sle, lulled somewhat by the fine weather of the trades, now began to respond to the strain of the doldrums. Quarrels flared into open breaks. Fists were raised and blows struck. The smallest slight was magnified into a grievance; the grievance smoldered into hate. There was, moreover, trouble on the poop. It was an open secret that the Old Man and the first mate were at logger-heads, the overweening masterfulness of the one striking sparks from the bad temper of the other. The mate, in addition to a brutality that exercised itself on all hands, was a shirker as well. And numerous times since the start of the voyage, he had been known to criticize his brother officers and even the Captain within hearing of the crew. The Old Man was forever finding fault with the trim of a yard or the stow of a sail, and relations between the two men were close upon an open break.

The mate vented his spite on the crew. Thus the atmosphere within the foc'sle was as uncertain and charged with electricity as was that of the poop. In the *Flying Cloud* Jeeter Sneed was always first to give voice to the dissatisfaction of the men. Who can say what were the forces that produced such a character as Sneed's? Spewed up out of the gutters of some seaport, the glitter of his eyes bespoke a nature that was as dangerous as dynamite. Ever since the day of our fight on the foc'sle head, we had avoided each other by unspoken assent, as much as possible within the narrow confines of a ship. But in those moments when we came, perforce, face to face, the malignancy of his look would have chilled a stouter heart than mine. I was ever on the watch, alow of aloft, if Sneed were within a fathom's length.

Due to his influence, the foc'sle of the *Cloud* seethed with currents and cross currents of suspicion and dissatisfaction. Invariably the weaker members of a crew are attracted to a leader of this sort, and it is usually a small thing that touches off the gunpowder that forms their composite mind.

As one day merged into another, caught within the exasperating grip of the doldrums, a party of malcontents began to form. Jeeter Sneed, assuming leadership, persuaded his followers that they were underpaid, underfed, over-worked, and generally abused. It was the food that brought affairs to a final crisis.

Returning from the galley one morning with his portion of "salt horse," Sneed shook it under the noses of his cronies in the foc'sle.

"Look at this bloody hunk o' granite!" he snarled. "A feller could carve a ship model out o' it if he had a knife keen enough!"

"Right you are, Matey," piped the shrill voice of Slim Harkins, who was Sneed's Prime Minister.

Swiftly Sneed turned upon the man. "Right I am, am I?" he mocked. "Well—why don't ye do something about it, then? If you jelly-livered sons o' perdition had an ounce o' blood in yer veins, ye'd stand up to the Old Man an' demand yer rights proper, like men!"

This was the tone of mutiny, sure enough, and it struck a responsive note in a score of breasts.

"We'd *orter* demand our blinkin' rights," echoed Slim Harkins. "Why should we break our ruddy necks to make money for the Owners when all we get out o' it is a fip-penny-bit? Let's up and at the Old Man and tell him what we think o' the way he runs this blasted barge; an' unless he mends his ways, we'll take over the ship ourselves and put in for South Ameriky!"

"Aye," assented Jeeter Sneed, "ther's gold there as well as in Californy, they say!"

"That's the idee!" sounded a new voice. "A drivelin' buzzard the Old Man is, snatchin' food out o' a pore sailor's belly! He'd orter be keelhauled proper!"

Captain Creesy saw the men coming and stopped in his stride.   Mister Andrews moved
out of stone, as prepared to m

e side of him, Mister Jones to the other. The Old Man stood there like a figure hacked
is hazard as all others.

Nils Olsen shouldered his hulk into the center of the crowd, his blue eyes crackling like Nordic ice. "Vot kind of sailors iss you men, yet?" he demanded. "Vot for you are talk such foolish? Dis iss mutiny! Ve vill haff no part in it!"

Only the power of his brawn saved him from being set upon. Sneed's eyes shifted before Olsen's and he turned back toward his henchmen, growling:

"We'll settle with your kind later!"

A bottle of rum passed around was all that was needed to fortify the faltering. A score of men marched aft with pannikins in hand and blood in their eyes. At the foot of the lee poop ladder they halted. In approaching the poop by the lee side, they were adding insult to injury, and they knew it.

Captain Creesy saw the men and stopped in his stride. Mister Andrews moved to one side of him, Mister Jones to the other. The Old Man stood there like a figure hacked out of stone, as prepared to meet this hazard as all others.

"Well, men!" he boomed, and his voice was terrible to hear. "What is the meaning of this?"

Slim Harkins, who had been elected spokesman while Jeeter Sneed reserved for himself the generalship of the men, was shoved forward. Slim paused at the foot of the ladder. He started to speak. He swallowed violently. What he saw in the Old Man's face struck terror in his soul. His carefully rehearsed string of complaints slipped from his wretched mind. Before the astonished eyes of his followers he collapsed like a burst balloon and ran for the foc'sle. A moment of panic all but stampeded the mutineers.

Jeeter Sneed leaped into the breech. He shouldered his way to the fore and thrust out his chin at the Captain.

"We'll have our rights, mister!" he shouted, lashing himself into a rage. His voice rose on a higher note as he yelled, "We ain't a-goin' to work no more unless——"

"Unless what, you scum!" came the Old Man's ominous voice.

"Unless we gets some proper food and——"

Sneed was in for it now. He could only go ahead. He started up the poop ladder. The Old Man stepped forward to meet him.

"Here's food for the likes o' you!" the Captain shouted, and the swing of his fist caught Sneed fair in the mouth.

The blow sent the man spinning backwards down the ladder. He struck the deck with a crash that seemed like to break his spine, but he leaped to his feet and turned toward his followers.

"Now's your chance!" he screamed at his men. "You blitherin' swine! After him! Get the ruddy buzzard!"

But the men, open-mouthed at the unexpected shape of events, turned to run for cover. The mates, armed with belaying pins, sprang after them. Blows rained thick and fast. Heads were cracked and men sprawled howling on the decks. Sneed, seeing his army collapse behind him, ran for the weather bulwark. He vaulted up to the rail and leaped into the ratlines. Mister Andrews started in pursuit, still armed with his belaying pin. Up the narrowing web of the shrouds Sneed fled with the mate at his heels. How he hoped to escape his fate no one could hazard. Panic held possession of him and he ran.

Looking upward we could see him swing out over the futtocks, in his haste almost missing his hold. Then into the maintop, scrambling toward the crosstrees. Now he was out upon the swaying yard. There, a rat brought to bay, he turned to face his pursuer.

"I'll have the law on you for this!" he screamed. "I'll——"

Like a ropewalker, Mister Andrews took the yard on a run while we below gasped and held our breath. We heard the blow of his belaying pin as it cracked against Sneed's skull. We saw the man's figure collapse; saw the mate, with unbelievable strength, grab the man by the neck as he fell, and drag him back to the crosstrees. Nils Olsen swarmed aloft to lend a hand carrying the inert figure down the shrouds.

Thus the mutiny ended, almost as it began. The perpetrators were rounded up and clapped in irons on hardtack and water. When Jeeter Sneed recovered from the blow dealt him by Mister Andrews, he found himself at the end of a yard of chain, ironed to a stanchion of the 'tweendecks. Then, as a general discipline for the rest of us, orders were given to shift our entire spread of sails. Two full days it took, with all hands on deck, and the mates saw to it that there was no "sogering." Roundly in our hearts we cursed Jeeter Sneed and his cronies. But for the first time in weeks I breathed freely. Now I was able to drop the vigilance that had dogged my days and nights.

*   *   *   *   *   *   *   *

We had picked up the southeast trades, and once more the *Flying Cloud* was whipping through the water under every

Up the narrowing web of the shrouds Sneed fled with the mate at his heels.

rag of canvas. With Sneed and his followers in irons, and fine weather prevailing again, good temper reigned in the foc'sle. The days slipped by like magic. At night new constellations were rising in the south while old familiar ones dropped in the north.

The *Flying Cloud* was on the larboard tack and her course was full and by; which meant that the helmsman steered by the wind and not by the compass. A simple enough job, as I found when it came my trick at the wheel. If the night were too dark to watch the upper sails and keep them lifting, I could hold the vessel to her course by the feel of the wind on my cheek.

While the mate napped in the lee of the poop, Brick and Lanny paused by the wheel and looked up at the night sky.

"The next time we clap an eye on the North Star," Brick observed, "we will have doubled the Horn and be standing to the nor'ard."

"Aye," agreed Lanny, "Old Tom Plunkett says that after you've rounded the Horn, the North Star is the first land you raise."

As I stood there at the wheel, giving her a spoke or two now and then, I wished that this voyage might never come to an end; that you and I, *Flying Cloud*, might clip through this blue element to watch a thousand days die in conflagration and a thousand nights sparkle with the friendly eyes of the stars.

CHAPTER VII

YARNS SPUN IN THE SECOND DOGWATCH—WE HEAR TELL
OF THE CORPOSANT

THE SECOND dogwatch, between six and eight of an
evening, belongs to the foc'sle. There's a sort of un-
written law of the sea that the men are given these two
hours of freedom for their own. On the *Flying Cloud* we
took full advantage of this custom during the fair weather of
the trades. It was a rest from the rigors behind us and a
breathing space in which to stiffen ourselves for the rough
work ahead, and we were grateful for it.

By this time Whit had become skilled with his concertina, and its rollicking tones beguiled the hours of the
second dogwatch, while the oldsters regaled the apprentices
with tales of their valor in the seven seas. Caleb Winthrop
was the accepted master of the chanteys. In the days when
every job aboard a ship was dependent upon human strength,
a chantey was like a jorum of rum to power a man's arm.
It was Caleb who "called" the songs, songs for hauling,

pumping, or heaving at the capstan. Graybeards those tunes were, some of them reaching back to the days of Drake himself; stirring music, too, with the swing of the sea in it:

> There was a ship—she sailed to Spain,
> There was a ship came home again.
>
> Oh, roll and go, my Johnny!
>
> What d'ye think was in her hold?
> There was diamonds, there was gold!
>
> Oh, roll and go, my Johnny!
>
> And what was in her lazareet?
> Good split peas and bad bull meat!
>
> Oh, roll and go, my Johnny!

Sometimes of an early evening, Brick and I, leaving the others on deck, would climb hand over hand to the upper rigging until at last we were sitting astride the royal yard. Below us the ship was lost in darkness. Whit's concertina seemed muted, while the lusty singing reached our ears, softened, like music from another sphere.

> They sang as only sailors sing
> Before the capstan bars;
> Or high amid the rigging for
> Their audience of stars!

The dark spires of the masts cut figures of eight across the sky. The stars hung so close that almost it seemed you could reach up and turn them off. Below us an acre of canvas swelled eerie-white in the darkness, while the trailing wake of the ship vanished in a glimmer of phosphorescence.

Sometimes of an early evening, Brick and I, leaving the others on deck, would climb hand over hand to the upper rigging until at last we were sitting astride the royal yard.

A few weeks ago I wouldn't have believed that I'd ever climb up here of my own accord. The wood of the great yards was still warm with the heat of the day. It felt almost alive under the grip of my hands. The creakings and murmurings of the ropes and spars wove their spell about me. The hush-hush from the cutwater whispered its song of the sea in my ear.

"You are alive, *Flying Cloud!* The wind is your breath of life! The sea is your pulse! How steadily it beats for you . . ."

With our feet hooked into the royal lifts and our legs swung fore and aft over the yard, Brick and I speculated upon many things.

"What do you suppose China'll be like, Brick?" I wondered.

"Mostly pigtails and pagodas, I cal'late, if you can believe the Chinese pictures."

"All yellow, I'll warrant: rivers and temples and men. Look! There's the Southern Cross! Rising later every night. Looks like a tipsy kite, hanging over on her side that way."

"Why they ever thought it looked like a cross is more'n I can see. There's Sirius!"

"Anybody could find that! It's the brightest one of all."

"All right then, m'lad. Let's see you locate Spica."

Together we scanned the heavens for a glimpse of Spica; a full ten minutes before we found her, pale as a ghost. Then we must search for Algol, flickering like a demon's fire; and Canopus, queen of the southern sky.

"What do you suppose tea looks like a-growing, and cinnamon and tapioca?"

"We'll know afore long now."

"Too bad we can't keep on going, right around the world, Brick."

"We'll do that next trip, Thach. We'll be Able Seamen then and any smart owners will be glad to sign us on! Gor, Thach!" he exulted suddenly, "this is the only life! Give me a cutlass and bring on your pirates and I'll slit them from clew to earring!"

On deck we found Tom Plunkett—better known as Chips—surrounded by a rapt audience, as he drew on a wheezing pipe and yarned of the old sea ways. Tom was a grizzled salt who had served his time before the mast in the East Indiamen and fought his way up through the Yankee hellships. At sixty-odd he was ruddy and clear of eye and his compact frame was as tough as the rock maple of the *Cloud's* keel. He was a past master of sea lore and a staunch believer in the ancient superstitions so close to the heart of all true sailormen.

Superstition seems as much a part of the ship herself as the water she sails in. It enters with the timber scarfed into her keel; it plays its part in her launch, her name, her days and hours of departure. As convoy on her voyages, it can promise good luck or ill; it can cause fair winds to blow, or foul. And when the time comes, it assures a port of rest off Fiddler's Green or in the grim locker of Davy Jones—as the case may be.

Old Tom drew on his pipe and looked cautiously around, lowering his voice the while.

"I had a hand in the building o' this-yere clipper," he whispered. "The builders had spoken a word for me, and, thinks I, if I'm a-goin' to sail in that-there ship, ther's two things I'm a-goin' to see to!"

We leaned forward, with ears apeak.

"What was that, Tom?" Lanny asked eagerly.

"Aye, Tom," the rest of us echoed, "tell us what it was."

Came a long draw on the pipe as Old Tom extracted full enjoyment from the center of the stage, then: "Wa-al, a bit o' stolen wood mortised into the keel makes a ship sail faster o' nights! I saw to that, though ther's naught as knows it and you lads can stow it under your hats."

This, I knew, was pure fiction, as the old man had boarded the *Cloud* in New York, and there laid eyes on her for the first time. But not for anything would I have discredited his tale, and it was good fun to draw him out.

"What was the second thing you did for the *Cloud?*" Brick queried.

Tom chuckled. "A silver coin placed in the mainmast step," came his answer. "Woe unto the ship, hearties, as weighs anchor wi'out that! She may make many a successful voyage, but Davy Jones'll lick her bones in the end."

Many other things he told us, some of which I had heard, others that were new to my ear. A black cat, he claimed, should not even be mentioned, for she carries a gale in her tail.

"An' never let me hear one o' you lads whistlin'!" he proclaimed. "It'll be keelhaulin' for *you*, I'll warrant! A proper Able Seaman, now, who's come up through the hawsepipe, can whistle to the blessed saints o' the sailor: San

We had picked up the southeast trades, and once more the *Flying Cloud* was whipping through the water under every rag of canvas.

Antonio or St. Nicholas—provided ther's a dead calm, that is. But not no apprentice, no sir!"

I had always heard that clergymen and women brought bad luck at sea, so I questioned Tom on the reasons for this particular notion.

"Humph!" he grunted in answer. "What else can a clergyman do aboard ship 'cept console the dyin' and bury the dead? Temptin' fate to carry 'em, I cal's it."

"But why should women bring bad luck at sea, Tom?"

The old man scratched his head with puzzled fingers, silenced for a moment.

"Wa-al," he said lamely, at last, "why else 'cept that— 'cept that the sea's the last place in the world for 'em!"

Tom hitched himself closer to us and lowered his voice till it was but a whisper. "As for that bo'sun," he muttered, "keep a weather eye on him! A Roosian, he calls himself, but I'm here to claim as he's a Roosian-Finn, and ther's naught worse aboard a ship. Should he stick his knife in a mast, hurricanes 'll dog us, and ca'ms beset, and we'll be lucky not to be lost on a lee shore. They brings bad luck to others, them Roosian-Finns, and good luck to theirsel's; their rum bottle is ne'er full nor empty, but always awash; and all they has to do is thrust a hand in their pocket, to produce a gold doubloon!"

These things Tom Plunkett told us not as a man relates a yarn, but as one who states a testament of faith. Thus he delivered, as actual occurrence, the story of the *Flying Dutchman:*

"Aye, that bloody Cape Horn we're bearin' down on is the ha'nt o' her," he muttered. "A ruddy Dutch windbag she were, with a blasphemin' heathen walkin' her poop. He tacked and he beat but he couldn't round the pitch o' the Cape, so what does he do but curse the blessed saints! Aye— can ye believe it? 'Tis a fact. And a proper reward he draws from 'em, too. They condemns him to keep on sailin' till the crack o' doom, wi'out e'er puttin' into port; wi' naught but gall to drink and red-hot iron to eat, and a watch to keep that will last till Jedgment Day."

"Did you ever see her, Tom?" Lanny asked breath-lessly.

"Aye, Tom, did you?"

"Nay." The old man shivered. "But once I were close enough to hear the sounds acomin' from her! Like the howlin' o' wolves, it were! Right off the pitch o' the Cape, too, and near enough in all truth, for it brought white squalls upon us, and tempests; and our rum soured and all our food turned to beans."

"I hope we don't run into——" began Whit, when the old man silenced him by clapping one paw over the lad's mouth.

"Don't speak on it!" he cried. "She's out there still, abeatin' and abeatin' into the eye o' the wind, wi' the stars shinin' through her sails, and them sounds o' howlin' comin' from her."

He snapped his jaw shut and puffed vigorously, and it was evident that he thought we had dwelt too long upon this dangerous subject. It took some minutes to beguile him into further discussion.

"Have you ever seen St. Elmo's Fire, Tom?" asked Brick.

"The *corposant?* Aye—and more than once! Last time was in the barque *Morning Star*, on a lee shore off Hatteras, and we knew not if we'd e'er lay eyes on our loved ones again. When suddenly, whiles the storm was at its blackest, I saw it twice: first, a small glitterin' ball o' fire at the masthead. Second, on the deck, bluish, like a star. And when I saw it, I tell ye lads, I shook like a gaff-tops'l in a squall! For death comes behind it, like a cart after a horse. That night the captain was washed off the poop and the second mate fell from the mainmast crosstrees, and it were only by the grace o' God that we e'er made port at all. Aye—I've seen it happen too often. Death follows in the wake of the *corposant!*"

In spite of ourselves we shivered. There was a depth of conviction behind the old man's statement that impressed itself upon the most skeptical of us. Small wonder, I reflected, that sailors are superstitious mortals: they must deal at first hand with that most unknowable of forces—the sea. The lonely nature of a life where ofttimes months pass without sight of another sail, gives rise to strange imaginings.

A gloom had settled upon us and, thinking to lighten it, Brick Warner hailed Ben Backstay.

"Ho, Ben!" he cried, "let's have that bowsing tale of yours about getting your walking papers in mid-ocean!"

Ben's one blue eye twinkled with fun. "What?" he chuckled, "you mean to say all you lads ain't never heerd 'bout the time I got my walkin' papers in mid-Pacific?" He cast his eye in Whit's direction. For Whit, being of solemn turn of mind and slow to catch the sparkle of a joke, was the sort of audience Ben Backstay relished most.

"Walking papers in mid-ocean?" demanded Whit, gulping the bait at a swallow. "Where could you walk to?"

"Wa-al, you see, m'lad, it was like this——" Ben settled back, scratched a match on the bowl of his pipe, and prepared to take his "two draws and a spit." The rest of us shifted closer, willing to bend an ear for as long as he should prove entertaining.

". . . It was when I was serving as cabin boy on the fine ship *Minervy* more years ago than the hull lot o' you could compute on yer fingers. We was fifty-two days out when it happened. Yes sir-ee, right in the middle o' the Pacific Ocean I got my walkin' papers. And it's one thing to get 'em served to you on *land*, where you got somethin' solid under yer pins; and still another to find yerself in the briny blue wi'out so much as a bit of plankin' to rest yer foot on."

"Come, git along with yer yarn, Ben," growled Caleb Winthrop. "This yawin' about is bad sailin'. Steer small and make a straight wake."

Ben cast a reproachful eye in Caleb's direction. "As I was sayin' afore bein' interrupted, it was a fine afternoon and the *Minervy* was friskin' along on a sou'westerly course. I had heerd the mate say as we was only about fifty miles from Galapagos Island. Long 'bout sundown the wind squalled up and we took in the r'yals and t'gant's. I was standin' on the weather side o' the foc'sle when all on a sudden I saw a porpoise rollin' along on top o' the water lookin' as cocky as you please. He sort-a walled one eye at me as much as to say: 'git yer hooks into *me*, if you can!' Wa-al, lads, he was a sight to tempt a hungry sailor, I tell you!

Since leavin' port we'd had no fresh food and I knew that porpoise could furnish a grand keel and upper works for a chowder.

"So—I ran to the longboat and got the harpoon and I clumb out on the bowsprit and down on the martingale stay before you could say Davy Jones. Along comes Mister Porpoise, friskin' his tail, right under my very feet. I let drive the harpoon wi' all my strength. A fine drive it were, too. Only—I *missed* him."

"Humph!" snorted Tom Plunkett. "How long d'you say you'd been to sea?"

"As I was sayin'," Ben continued imperviously, "by some ill chance, I missed him. And not having took the precaution of makin' a turn wi' the rope that was fastened to the harpoon, I lost my foothold and splashed into the sea. With a great churning and a grinding the ship passed right over me. When I shook the water out o' my eyes and caught my breath, there was the *Minervy*, halfway out on the horizon. And though I blew like a grampus and bellowed like a bull no one on that ruddy ship heerd me. Night was settlin' down by now and in no time the *Minervy* was lost to sight.

"I began to take stock o' the situation and it looked like there was plenty o' room for improvement. I still had hold of the harpoon, and the wooden shaft supported me somewhat. The moon was comin' up and I took a squint around in the hopes that they might ha' missed me on the *Minervy* by this time, and put about. But nary a solitary thing but water and sky and my own lone self!

"All on a sudden I spied a dark-lookin' somethin' floatin' on the water not a cable's length away. What could it be? My heart quicked a beat, I can tell ye, as it drifted toward me, and I took a good grip on my harpoon. And what do you lads think it was?" Ben paused with good effect.

Of one accord we demanded: "What?"

"A loggerhead turtle! One o' them Galapagos boys. Sound asleep on top o' the water he was, too. He must ha' been a good six foot long and I'll lay a wager he weighed five hundred pounds. I knew then that Providence hadn't altogether deserted a pore sailor. I made up my mind that that turtle should take me in tow! I knew that Galapagos must lie somewhere's to the east, for the wind had been blowin' out o' the west, and I knew that the current sets nearly due east in the Pacific when near the Equator. (And a mighty good thing it will be for some o' you lads to l'arn these things, in case you should ever be in such a preedicament as I was!) Wa-al, as I was sayin', I figgered that that logger-head orter give me a tow to Galapagos, where I could pick up some vessel for home or the Indies. So I paddled gently towards him and swam up under his stern. Wi' one hand I threw the bite o' the harpoon line over his head, and with t'other I grabbed him by the tail.

"Well, sir—that turtle awoke with a bang! If I hadn't been onto the tricks o' them fellers, I'd ha' been in a bad way. He had no idee, o' course, what manner o' critter had him by the tail, so his first panic prompted him to a plunge. I was ready for him. I seized onto his rear flippers and bore down on 'em wi' all my weight. For the life o' him he couldn't get his blinkin' head under, much less his clumsy hulk. So off he went, at a good six knots, towin' me after him! By pushin' at one flipper and pullin' on t'other I

The single peak that crowned the little island reared like a gigantic finger, warning us
cold and s

ware the sterner seas to the south.   Scarce had we dropped it astern when the nights fell shivering.

managed to steer a course due east, near as I could jedge from the bearin' o' the moon.

"But bein' dragged through the water by a ruddy turtle ain't all beer and skittles. When finally I was about tuckered and wonderin' how much longer I could hold out, what do I see but the dark shape o' land off my starboard bows. Galapagos! And ne'er was a glimpse o' *terra firma* more welcome to a mariner after an eight-months' passage from Chiny. The only thing I was a-feared of now was that Mister Loggerhead would tire out afore he reached land, 'cause he was a-breathin' hard by this time, I can tell you. But no sir-ee. He beached me right and proper on the shores o' Galapagos. And I clumb up out o' reach o' the surf and lay me down on the sand and slept like the dead till the sun waked me up.

"And jest as I was a-thinkin' that I'd ha' been better off in the sea than on that wild strip o' shore, I got the second surprise o' my life. What do you lads think I saw?"

"What?" we breathed.

"The *Minervy!* Yep! Anchored right out in the bay. Seems like she'd sprung a leak about her rudderpost and put in to Galapagos fer repairs. And were my shipmates *astonished* to see Ben Backstay alive and in the flesh! Put out they was, too, because already they'd divvied up my belongings amongst 'em."

"Well—it *is* an astonishing story, and that's a fact," acknowledged Whit solemnly. "But are you sure it's all—true, Ben?"

Ben bit off half a fathom of Irish Twist and his one blue eye was filled with reproach as he turned it upon Whit.

"Every word as true as *Bowditch's Navigator*, and you can lay to that!" he swore.

* * * * * * * *

All hands were working now in anticipation of the gales and seas of the Roaring Forties. In the watch below, the older men were getting their gear in shape for the bleak weather ahead. Oilskins were being tarred and mended; sea boots repaired, holes patched wherever needed, and woolen underclothes darned. For Jack can ply a skilful needle when there is no woman to do it for him.

Our watches on deck were spent in unbending the old sails and bending on the newest and best. Contrary to the custom of the landsman, a ship puts on her best rig for rough weather and saves her poorest for the milder breezes of the trades. The *Cloud* was stripped of her top hamper; her skys'l and royal yards sent down. With her t'gant's still crossed, she was made ready for the rough-and-tumble work ahead. The seas were greener now and more stubborn. They rolled up under the stem of the *Flying Cloud* as if they would shoulder her back from her course. The skies took on a sterner tinge.

A cry of "Land Ho-o-o-!" from the masthead brought us all on deck at a bound.

The little island of South Trinidad, miles out at sea from the Brazilian coast, lay on our larboard bow; the first bit of land we had raised since sailing out of New York harbor. Through the spyglass that old Messina Clarke had given me, I examined this, my first island. A wilder, more romantic bit of land would be hard to find: lofty and sea-scarred, with waterfalls leaping from the cliffs to bury

themselves in the jungle below; surf smashing with a mighty thunder on the barrier reef. Here pirates are said to have fled with the plunder of Peru, and this was easy to credit. What pictures it painted before the eye, of buccaneers with flashing cutlass; of doubloons and ambuscadoes and jeweled loot lying five fathoms deep!

The single peak that crowned the island reared like a gigantic finger, warning us to beware the sterner seas to the south. Scarce had we dropped it astern, when the nights fell cold and set us shivering.

When the day came that we had seen the last of the flying fish, we knew that we were in the region of the Great Westerlies.

CHAPTER VIII

THE *Flying Cloud* IN THE ROARING FORTIES—WE SEE THE
CORPOSANT—TRAGEDY OFF CAPE HORN

THE *Flying Cloud* was in the Roaring Forties, running
down her easting. Here, for nine months of the year,
the Great Westerlies blow true to their name. Their direction never varies but their strength rises gradually to hurricane fury. For thousands of miles there is nothing to stay
their force nor deflect the driving power of the league-long seas.

We were running with our lee rails under. It was a
quartering sea that held little threat and the Old Man
crowded canvas on the *Cloud* till she fled like a deer with the
wolves at her heels. Day after day when the log was hove
she was reeling a full fifteen knots, and the man holding the
reel was put to it to keep his arm from being jerked from
its socket.

But suddenly, with the crossing of the 45th parallel,
the weather broke up. The cold became more searching.
All day the wind had been stiffening and a dirty sea was
making. The ship was still wearing everything but her
royals, staggering now under the tremendous press of canvas.
The mate, wedged into a corner of the monkey rail, let her
drive. We apprentices had been literally drowned out of
our half deck and forced to take up our quarters in the
foc'sle with the rest of the crew. The older men clumped

125

below, cursing the mate for not reefing the t'gant's when the watch was changed, delaying it in order to call "all hands!" and thus ruin a watch below.

"Might as well set up and stay awake," growled Caleb Winthrop. "Small use goin' to sleep jest to be woke up agin."

"He'll have the sticks out o' her afore long, mark my words," grumbled Ben Backstay. "Showin' off, that's what he's doin'. Ain't he never goin' to take in them t'gant's?"

"Nobody'd care if 'twas a proper hurricane," complained Caleb. "But the old fule makes a hurricane hazard out o' an ordinary gale by carryin' twice the canvas a single watch can handle. Blast his boots and breeches!"

Herded. together in the sodden foc'sle with only the thickness of a few planks between them and the outer activity, the trained ear of the old salt deciphered each sound from aloft. The sudden whip of canvas and the grunting cries of men hauling on the clew lines told them that the t'gans'ls were finally coming in.

"'Bout time, too!" they grumbled.

The smoking oil lamp swung in its gimbal with every pitch and roll of the ship, only a small area of the foc'sle being lighted by its dim glow; the rest was lost in darkness as deep as the gloom that settled upon our spirits. There was no heat in the foc'sle and no means of drying our clothes. Most of the men turned into their bunks without even removing their oilskins. Others, with more courage than logic, stripped and wrung the water out of their clothes and wrapped themselves up in their wet blankets. The howl of the wind was all about us. The whole ship shuddered under the impact of the seas that struck at her over the weather bulwark.

We huddled there in our bunks or perched on our sea chests, awaiting the return of Zeke Rilling, who had volunteered to wheedle Doctor into making some hot coffee. None of us liked Rilling but we hoped for our stomach's sake he would be successful. We hated him because he was a bully who, like most of his breed, was a coward at heart. But the bluster of his bellow and the massive power of his shoulders held back all but the more intrepid from crossing his wake. He seemed to take special pleasure in taunting Marat, a diminutive Frenchman. Marat, who was a splendid sailor, had a sharp tongue and the explosive nature of so many of his race. It was known that he carried a knife against his lean ribs and we all feared that one day, when Rilling should have goaded him beyond endurance, there would be blood shed.

"I tell ye, I'm through wi' ships!" muttered Ben Backstay, wringing the water out of his beard and trying to dry his pipe over the smoking lamp chimney. "When a man reaches my time o' life, he'd orter be settin' in front o' the fire, fillin' his pipe and his bread basket. Here I am, froze to the marra', eatin' dog food and gettin' no more sleep than a nervous cat. 'Tain't right, I'm tellin' ye, fer a man o' my years! I'm through wi' the sea! Once I set my foot ashore again, I'm a-goin' to raise beans and pertaters till Gabriel sounds the horn." He spat with an air of finality. We all knew that he had been swearing this promise for forty years.

The door banged open. Against the pale rectangle of light we could see Zeke Rilling—empty-handed. No hot coffee. We groaned. A sea smashed against the bulwark and its overflow piled into the foc'sle through the open door and raced across the floor, taking oilskins, pannikins, and whatnot in its wake.

"Shut zat door!" screamed Marat, beside himself with Latin fury.

The utter wretchedness of our plight, our chilled bodies, our empty stomachs, our broken fitful slumber, seemed to have brought to a climax something seething in the little Frenchman's soul. That Zeke Rilling, his hated tormentor, should have brought about this climax was an irony in keeping with their antagonism.

Deliberately Rilling held the door open. Another sea swept into the foc'sle, filling the bunk on the lee side of the door and leaving us all standing in a foot of water.

"Come on, Zeke," growled Olsen. "Shut dot door."

Zeke Rilling slammed the door and strode over to the circle of light, under which Marat crouched on his sea chest.

"An' who do ye think *you* are, givin' *me* orders!" he snarled. "I'm a mind to smarten you up with the weight o' my fist, you dirty little frog!"

Marat rose from his sea chest. There was something so ominous in his movement that we held our breath. No man made a sound. For a second it seemed that even the elements had paused to listen. The light from the lamp flickered over the two figures. It picked them out of darkness and left them standing on the edge of an abyss. Neither man would ever be the same after this moment.

"Dirty leetle frog, am I!" Marat's voice was edged like a blade. Suddenly it rose to a scream. "Take *zat* from a frog!"

Like a flash of light he leaped and drove both his feet low into Rilling's belly. Zeke Rilling staggered and all but lost his footing, while a grunt of pain broke from his lips. He straightened up and glowered at Marat. The rest of us stood there, rooted, waiting to see murder done. But Marat knew his man. He swaggered up to the bully whose hulk towered above him so that he had to throw back his head to fling his taunt in the man's teeth.

"*Eh bien!* Meester Rilling!" he jeered. "Why you no fight? Afraid of ze leetle frog, eh?"

Zeke Rilling seemed to collapse. He backed away from the Frenchman, stumbled over the sea chest, and fell sprawling on the sodden bunk behind him. He buried his head and sobbed like a child. The rest of us were suddenly embarrassed, as if we had witnessed some murky secret of a man's soul that should be hidden from all eyes but his own; and we busied ourselves with our sea boots and lashed oilskins about our bodies.

The door banged open, filling the foc'sle with the outer thunder, while a voice roared:

"All hands on deck! Lay to it, mates. There's the devil to pay aloft!"

When we hit the deck, we knew that we were in for it. Rain edged with ice added its hum to the song of the elements. All around was tumult: groaning timber, the whine of taut rope, the rattle of the chain sheets. Above all was the thunder of the breasting seas as they broke over the weather bows and

rushed aft along the submerged bulwarks. We dodged along the deck in the lee of the weather rail, trying to get aft without a ducking. Luck was with us. We made the poop ladder without being overtaken by an inrushing sea and we ran for the shelter of the lee alleyway. The larboard watch was waiting for us, cursing us for our slowness in relieving them. They moved toward the ladder as if the very joints of their bones were frozen.

There came a crack from for'ard like a volley of shot— then the mighty cannonading of blown-out canvas.

"The foretops'l!" cried a voice.

In the darkness we could make out the canvas split to ribbons, torn from the bolt ropes, and borne off on the wind.

"Foretops'l hal'ards!" bellowed the mate. "Tail onto it, you blasted lubbers! What're you waitin' for?"

Cursing and fumbling in the darkness, we sprang for the halyards and the yard came down on the run. The Old Man appeared on the poop and the order was given to furl the main tops'l. The command, shouted above the wind by the Old Man, was snapped up by the mates and flung at the men.

"Call all hands, Thacher!" barked Mister Andrews.

I clawed my way to the foc'sle door and flung it open to shout into the darkness:

"All hands to shorten sail!"

A chorus of groans and imprecations was hurled at me as the watch below came tumbling out, without having closed an eye. The maintops'l was lowered; the great yard braced to spill the sheet, stiff and heavy with ice. It blew straight out from the yard with a thunder like the salvo of frigate guns, fighting to tear itself loose from the stops that held it. Then it was "aloft and furl!"

The force of the wind flattened us to the ratlines as we made our way up the rigging. Now we were out on the plunging yard, scarce able to see one another for the darkness. Over the yard on our straining bellies, beating at the sail with numb fists; gathering it up, inch by bitter inch; mastering it. Half an hour later we slithered down the shrouds and fought our way aft to the Mate's call of "grog ho!"

Dawn was no more than a grayish lightening of the skies to the east. Through a narrow rent in the heavens a gleam of yellow bespoke the fact that a sun still rose in this tumbling world. Now the first of the albatross brought us a Cape Horn greeting. From the upper Patagonian coast on the Atlantic to the same latitude on the Pacific, these birds form a ship's convoy in sunshine or whistling gale. White miracles of grace they are, snowy-breasted, with slate markings on their wide wings. Their flight is a fascination to the eye, for the stiffer the wind the more supreme seems the albatross's mastery of the air. They float and wheel on wings wide-spread and motionless save for a scarcely perceptible tilt to lift or lower their elevation. They can run athwart a gale of eighty-mile velocity, take it head-on, or hang suspended without apparent effort. As they swept low at the masthead, turning their gentle eyes upon us, they seemed to testify to the notion of the old shellbacks who claimed that their bodies housed the souls of drowned sailors and, if killed, the wandering ghost would bring disaster upon him who caused it.

The older men eyed them with respect and not without affection, but they frowned at the first of "Mother Carey's chickens," as they called the stormy petrels. Amusing little fellows these, in mottled jackets of black and white; they darted over the surface of the sea with quick, flitting movement, their slim, trailing legs making them seem almost to be walking upon the water. They were believed to bring dirty weather in their wake, which accounted for their connection with Mother Carey—a mythical old woman of evil reputation. Watching them dart and flicker over the tumbling seas, Tom Plunkett shook his head wisely. "Ole Cape Stiff's jest around the corner!" he warned.

The mutineers, whose services were now sorely needed, were released from their irons in the 'tweendecks, with the understanding that they would be dealt with when the proper time came. Jeeter Sneed, deemed the most dangerous, was left at the end of his yard of chain where it was ironed to the 'tweendeck's stanchion. Here he daily hurled curses at the steward who brought him his hardtack and water.

*   *   *   *   *   *   *   *

Cape Horn. Black-named, and deserving it. Region of hurricane gales and rain; of sleet and hail and snow; of league-long rollers sweeping up from the Antarctic to break their backs on the coast of Tierra del Fuego. On the ship, days of lowering darkness through which the sun never penetrated, an endless cycle of work—work in icy water, with frozen hands split to the bone, trying to snug sail in driving squalls of snow and sleet; the ropes heavy with ice, swelling in the throats of the blocks.

The *Flying Cloud* was driving along under Cape Horn canvas: double-reefed tops'ls, fores'l and jib. The helmsmen were lashed to the wheel, fighting it. The Old Man was braced beside them on the poop, an anxious furrow between his eyes. A green ship, the *Flying Cloud*, untried as yet by the Horn. How much would she stand? That jib—ought to have come in. She was hard-mouthed and bucking the men at the wheel. But it so frequently occurred that a gale, blowing itself out toward night, dictated a need for shortening sail when that need was past. The Old Man decided that he would let her rip! So rip it was! But Cape Stiff had a trick up her sleeve: the gale didn't blow itself out with nightfall; it freshened. The *Cloud* yawed, and scooped up a thousand tons of green water that smashed at hatch combings and capstans and foc'sle as if it would have destroyed them if it could. Even the life lines stretched along her main deck were hazardous for a man to trust his life to. From horizon to horizon the graybeards swept— mountains moving, invincible, inexorable.

Still the gale freshened in sudden squalls of blasting fury. The seas were mounting; black walls of water whose crests were torn off by the wind and flung into the valleys. They loomed above us, beside us, behind us. They rolled aboard,

ready to smash, to kill. It was stand-by for both watches and sleep for none.

"Zat *cochon* of a capitaine! He weel kill us all!" cursed Marat savagely. "What for he does not heave-to?"

But heaving-to was out of the question. To have brought the *Cloud* broadside to those seas, even for one second, would have spelled the end for us all. There was naught to do but let her drive. We were huddled on the weather side of the poop, clinging to the rigging and life lines. A splintering crash at my elbow caused me all but to lose my grip: where the stern lifeboat had swung from its davits a second before, there was now only empty space; the davits were bent double, the chocks empty, the lashings rent.

Looking upward, we saw a ghastly phenomenon: from the boom iron of the straining maintops'l yard, a bluish ball of fire paled and flickered. We watched it, tranced with awful fascination, as it moved to the end of the weather yard and vanished in the darkness. The *corposant!* I found myself shivering with an ague that was like to loose my very teeth from their moorings.

"Lay out there and furl the jib!"

The long-expected order—the most dangerous sail on a ship to stow. The footropes of the jib boom on which a man must stand hang directly over the sea.

"Out with you, you shiverin' jellyfish!"

The mate's voice lashed at us like a whip. Nils Olsen, Brick Warner, and I were nearest to him. With a kick and a shove he propelled us toward the ladder. We crouched for a second, waiting to make a dash for it. Seas were crashing aboard with every roll. Now! We clawed our way across

the slippery deck. The foc'sle head. . . . Waves slopped over and cracked like thunder behind us as we ran. We climbed between the knightheads and out upon the rearing bowsprit; feet feeling in the darkness for the swaying foot-rope; holding on by a spar and the grace of God.

One moment we were lifted skyward, clinging like limpets to whatever we could hook our fingers into. The next— plunged waist deep in icy water. We worked with the frenzy of the mad. Numb fingers fumbled with the gaskets. Cries tore from our lips, whipped away on the wind.

A wave was looming just ahead, livid, monstrous. . . . Out of the clew of my eye I saw it coming. Nils yelled a warning. Brick, on the end of the boom didn't hear. I screamed to him at the top of my lungs. The wind shoved my voice down my throat. The wave rushed at us. Blindly I buried my head—wove myself around rope and boom.

The wave struck. The ship trembled to her keel bolts. Stunned, gasping, I felt myself being dragged from my hold. It was Nils' hand grabbing me by the collar, hauling me to the safety of the knightheads. Brick—I looked back. Brick was gone. Ah, God!

"*Man overboard! Man overboard!*" shrilled the cry.

Then madness let loose. Men clawing their way from aft.

"Rope! Rope, you fools!"

Somewhere out in that trap of black water was Brick. Good old Brick. Shouts, imploring, entreating, tore from a hundred throats.

"Brick! Brick! A rope! Lay hold!"

"Where are you, Brick? Where——"

Orders cracked through the air. Sail had been slacked somehow. Ropes thrashed in wild tangle about the decks.

"There he is! There—see!"

"Brick! Look—a rope!"

Brick's head appeared for a second in the foam, close beside the ship. A terrible fear was in his eyes. A wave was rising above him. A giant among giants. A cliff of smoking water. It would sweep him away past all hope of rescue. His hands clutched at a rope—closed spasmodically. The wave broke. The wind shrilled a fiercer note. A cry went up from the men.

Brick was gone.

*   *   *   *   *   *   *   *

Hours passed . . . days . . . all sense of time was lost. Only ice and sea and wind and stubborn canvas. Frozen hands, frozen brains. A ship plunging, fighting for life. One man, the Captain, meeting the sea as an equal: his skill against the ocean's might. The rest of us were sunk in misery. Somehow we got through our tasks, carried out orders that seemed beyond human possibility, while through our minds the words of Tom Plunkett tolled like a bell:

"The *corposant*? Aye, death comes behind it like a cart after a horse!"

For more than forty-eight hours the Old Man had not left the poop, except to go below to glance at the barometer or warm the chill in his veins with a pot of hot coffee. He stood braced beside the helmsmen, gray and haggard; silent save to issue an order. There was something timeless and inevitable about him as he stood there, grim with cold, master of his ship and his men; alone in the isolation that is the stuff

"Go ahead then!" the mate yelled, beside himself by now. "Remove me from duty! I'm si

killing myself for naught.   This ship was never built for these seas, and the men know it!"

of command.   Many times since the start of the voyage he
had been raked by the criticism of the foc'sle, and even by
his own first mate.   But no man seeing him now felt aught
but admiration for him as he stood there, conning his ship
by the sweep of the sea.   He was a figure hewn out of marble.
The life of every one of us depended upon his judgment,
his knowledge, his "sixth sense" of the true mariner that
warned him how much this balanced fabric of wood and
canvas would stand without parting.

It was this very day that brought his relations with the
first mate to a crisis.   There came a momentary lull in the
storm when the Old Man went below for a cat nap.   His
steward had broken an arm and Mister Andrews detailed me
to fetch a pot of coffee from the Doctor and take it to the
Captain.   As I stepped into the corridor outside his door,
I heard angry voices issuing from within: the Old Man's
and the Mate's.

"The Falklands are only three hundred miles to the
west of us," the mate was saying.   "Take my advice and
run for them!"

"*Your* advice!" the Old Man roared.   "You overreach
yourself, mister!"

"Yes, *my* advice!" the mate shouted.   "The men are
done in, I tell you.   You'll have a *real* mutiny on your hands
this time!   This bloody ship was never built for these seas
and they know it.   It's a simple matter to put in at the
Falklands and wait for this cursed gale to blow itself out."

"Mister Jones, mark this!"   And the Old Man's voice
was terrible to hear.   "We are doubling the Horn and standing for 'Frisco!   I've put up with a goodly bit from you since

we cleared port. You've shirked your duties abominably, sir, and criticized the other officers and myself within hearing of the men. Now tail onto this: the least sign of insubordination from you in the future and I will remove you from duty and see that you get your desserts when we reach California!"

"Go ahead then!" the mate yelled, beside himself by now. "Remove me from duty! I'm sick of killing myself for naught! I tell you we're never going to get around the Horn!"

"Get to your cabin!" thundered the Old Man.

The door flung open so violently before the mate's departure that I was like to be knocked spinning, coffeepot and all.

"Thacher!" bellowed the Captain, "send Chips here with a padlock and a hammer!"

The *Cloud* was laboring under the weight of water on her decks, unable to shake herself free of one sea before another raced aboard. I fought my way for'ard to fetch Chips, speculating upon the outcome of this new development between the Captain and his first mate, and wondering what Jonah had signed the ship's articles.

I looked up to see a wave curling above me over the weather bulwark, almost upon me. Through my mind flashed an old warning of the mate's: never run from a sea— grab hold of anything you can find and hang on. Blindly I looked . . . there was nothing. I turned and ran for the poop ladder. The wave cracked like a pistol shot. Water, icy, relentless, rushed up to my stomach, swelled under the legs of my oilskins, and poured into my sea boots. I staggered

and fell.   Another sea sheeted over, bigger than the first.
I tried to rise.   It swept me away.   Overboard?   Where
was I?   Out in that black maelstrom where no man might
see the light of day?   What an end to life—to drown like a
foc'sle rat.   There was my mother's face, twisted with grief
. . . Messina Clarke, holding out a hand . . . Donald McKay,
watching, speechless . . .

Where was I?

The wave flung me against the poop ladder.   It left me
there, wrenched in every bone.   I crawled to my feet, filled
now with a blind, reasonless rage.   I shook my fists at the
sea.   Sobs tore at my throat as I cursed it.

". . . You bloody sea!   You've destroyed Brick!   Now
you're trying to destroy the *Flying Cloud!*   My ship!   Well
—you shall not, Sea!   Do you hear?   *You shall not! . . .*"

Though I shouted with all my power, no sound could
I hear of my own voice.   The seas swept by with unfalter-
ing swing.

Lanny brought back the news from his trick at the
wheel that we were off the pitch of the Cape.   The *Cloud*
was stripped to double-reefed tops'ls on the fore and main.
It was all that she could stagger under and it seemed as if
bare sticks would have been enough.   Only those two squares
of canvas, drum-tight. . . . The wild swing of the compass
card rendered it useless, and throughout the day the Old
Man conned his ship by the sweep of the seas.   From horizon
to horizon the ocean was one vast mountain range moving
in wild flight.   As the *Cloud* slithered down some smoking
slope into a yawning hollow, the water ahead loomed higher
than her foreyard.   The next second her bows were surging

toward the sky, while her poop sank into the trough and a cliff of toppling water rose up behind. It was a sight to try the hardiest soul to look astern and see a wall of hissing water rolling up above the taffrail, thirty, forty feet. When it seemed that it must certainly overwhelm the ship, she slipped from beneath it with a fathom to spare and the water rushed forward under her counter.

There was no chance now to wear or heave-to. If she fell off for one second into the trough of those thundering seas, we were lost. Nothing to do but let her drive. The men of both watches huddled on the poop. No orders to carry out while the gear held. Nils Olsen and Caleb Winthrop, the best wheelsmen, were lashed to the helm. The Old Man stood braced beside them. The place of the first mate, locked in his cabin, was filled by the second. It was impossible to light a fire in the galley, and at midday we washed down sea biscuit with cold water. The main deck was swept constantly by tons of water. A dash for'ard was a matter of life and death.

As the murky light of day thickened with approaching night, we saw a monstrous wave rolling up astern. Many we had seen, but this appeared the veritable grandfather of the giants. It bore down down upon us with unapposable stride. The *Cloud*, weighted under her burden of water, lay inert, as if she sensed this new attack and lacked the strength to combat it.

Of all the disasters that can overtake a ship, there is none more terrifying than being pooped: a running ship over-reached by a following sea. Any other part of a ship may be submerged, but her stern is her head and it must not go under.

The Old Man threw a backward glance over his shoulder and shouted:

"Let everything stand! Into the rigging, men! Hang on for your lives!"

He leaped to the wheel beside the tense wheelsmen. The rest of us sprang into the rigging and swarmed up the ratlines to the maintop.

The wave was upon us. High above the taffrail it hung, fifty, sixty feet, wiping out the sky. The *Cloud* slid down into an awful hollow. High as the ends of the lower yard-arms the crest curled over with a mighty hiss. Down it crashed. Chaos. Water rushed forward in a cataract of thunder. Everything was swept before it. It was the end of a world. Clinging to the backstays ten feet above the poop, I was all but torn from my hold.

"My God! We're done!" I heard a voice cry.

As my head cleared, I looked downward. The entire ship was submerged, nothing visible but her careening spars with dots of men clinging like limpets to her rigging. The sea that had pooped us left disaster in its wake. The compass and binnacle had disappeared. I saw Nils Olsen and the Old Man clinging, by some miracle, to the wheel; Caleb Winthrop jammed under the smashed wheel box. The poop was swept clean; the cabin skylight smashed to kindling and tons of water pouring into the cabin below.

The wheelsmen were fighting to keep the *Cloud* from broaching-to. With the acuteness of perception that in moments of chaos makes us notice insignificant things, I saw the veins knotting on their foreheads and the white strain of their knuckles. Another sea was rearing astern of us. We could see it coming. A voice cried, "We're done for!"

Would the *Cloud* rise? We could not say. The Old Man could not say. Only God knew. Another bucket of water would finish her.

The wave was almost upon her. . . . Slowly, tiredly, the *Flying Cloud* shook herself. Water poured out through her scuppers. Free of its weight she rallied. For one second the wave hung. We watched, tranced with a sense of doom. Then—her stern lifted to it! A hoarse cheer tore from the throats of a hundred weary men.

All through that wild night we drove. But the worst was over. Toward dawn the gale moderated. The *Flying Cloud* had rounded the pitch of the Cape and started the long Pacific slant northward. The seas roared aboard no longer. Life lines were unrigged and reefs shaken out; the t'gans'ls set; the royal and skys'l yards crossed once again.

But that sense of the hostility and might of the sea lay heavy on us still. Something fine and bright had gone out from the world.

Brick was gone.

CHAPTER IX

THE PACIFIC SLANT—WHALES—I REMEMBER A VOW

S AIL Ho-o-o-!"

The call from the lookout had an electrifying effect. The first sign of human life that the *Flying Cloud* had raised in fifty-four days. We rushed to the bulwarks, sprang into the ratlines, swarmed aloft, each one of us eager to be the first to see the ship.

"There she is! Larboard quarter!"

A brig, riding solidly on the long glassy swells. Signals were exchanged and we found that she was the *Catawba* out of Nantucket, Captain Obed Swain, master. A whaleship— but the sturdy cut of her had already decided that, even before signal and spyglass settled the point.

For several days we had seen sperm whales, moving rapidly, always to windward. Now and then a finback and several right whales. And wherever whales are, there will you find the New England whaler going about his dangerous job in the most matter-of-fact manner possible. The wind had fallen to a dead calm. It was one of those immaculately clear days at sea, without a cloud in the sky or hint of mist in the air, and as we drifted toward the *Catawba*, we could see the men perched in her rigging and hear their voices in eager debate about the *Flying Cloud*.

The Old Man ordered a boat lowered. He meant to be rowed over to the whaleship to pass an hour or two with her commander, and I counted myself lucky when Mister Andrews gave me the word to swing down to one of the oars and bend my back with Lanny and Olsen and Caleb Winthrop.

The Old Man sat in the stern sheets, and despite his expressionless face, we knew that he was as anxious as we to exchange news and break the monotony of the days with this diversion. We rowed up under the counter of the *Catawba*, made fast, then swarmed up on the deck where Captain Swain stood waiting to greet our commander. The two men went below to the cabin to yarn, while the rest of us were surrounded by members of the whaleship's crew, who plied us for tobacco and asked all manner of questions. They had never laid eyes on a clipper of the *Flying Cloud's* magnitude and they wanted to know all about her from A to Zed.

A sudden cry from the lookout at the masthead threw the ship into turmoil and brought an end to their curiosity.

"Thar sh'blows! Blo-o-ws!" sounded the cry.

The door of the companionway banged open before Captain Swain, followed by the Old Man. The commander of the *Catawba* hurled orders at his mates. The mates hooked curses to the orders and flung them at the men.

"Ah blo-o-ws! Blo-o-ws!"

Looking upward, I saw atop the mainmast of the whaler a curious contrivance, the like of which appears on no other type of ship: a small platform surmounted by two iron hoops fastened to the mast, at the height of a man's stomach. Here the lookout must stand through the weary hours of his watch.

"Where away?" shouted the Captain.

"Two points off the lee bow! Blows sperm whales!"

Of one accord we rushed to the bulwarks. Not a quarter mile off we saw a sudden heaving to the surface of a glistening black bulk, and a jet of vapor thrown high into the air.

The mate was training his spyglass on the scene. "Blows about a quarter mile off, sir," he announced. "And coming to wind'ard."

"Call all hands!" shouted the Captain. "Back yer main yard! Get yer boats ready, mister."

At the first cry from the lookout, the crew had stripped off their shirts and shoes and taken a double reef in their belts as they prepared for the work at hand. The crews of whaleships have come in for so much blackguarding that here I would like to discredit a current belief concerning them, so far as lies within my power. It is a fact and true that whalemen were a rougher lot than the men encountered in the merchant service. There is no gainsaying that ashore their conduct was ofttimes lamentable and such as to cast a dark light of public disfavor upon them. But within their own realm, the sea, I wish here to state that no finer body of men ever lived or breathed. Strong, courageous, fearless; ready to face any personal hazard in pursuit of their profession; they were men of iron will and stout heart and, taken by and large, a credit to the sea they followed.

"Stern all!" yelled the mate, and the boat was instantly oared backward to
clear the whale.

However imperfectly disciplined they may be, a system of order prevailed on the *Catawba*—as on all ships of the whaling type—and in two shakes of a rope yarn the confusion on deck had straightened itself out. The men stood poised and ready to swing themselves over the side and into the lowered whaleboat.

The Captain indicated the boat he wished to attack the whale. The boat header and the harpooner took their stations in bow and stern while it was yet hanging in the davits.

"Clear away that larboard boat!" shouted Captain Swain. "Here, Chips, lend a hand with them davy-tackles. Ready? Hoist and swing!"

The davit tackles were run out by the men on deck and the boat dropped to the water with a smart splash, while the oarsmen swung over the ship's rail and tumbled into their positions almost by the time the whaleboat had slapped the water. Each man knew his proper place. In spite of the appearance of a mad scramble, there was no confusion. For more than two centuries the manner of killing whales has been preserved intact; the method of boarding a whale, the instruments to be used, the position of the boats and the number of men in them, all are dictated by long precedent and never varied. A tradition has been established.

The mate in the stern sheets barked at his men: "Out oars! Pull ahead! Clear of the ship, now—that's well!"

From the poop the Captain shouted, "Cut in ahead of the whale if you can, mister!"

"Come on, b'ys! Bend yer backs!" the mate bellowed. "That fellow's got a hundred barrels of ile under his ribs, if he's got a gill!"

Clinging to the ratlines of the *Catawba* we could see the whaleboat dancing over the waves toward its quarry. We could see the glistening black hulk of the whale, as long as the *Catawba* itself, lying on the surface; feeding perhaps, and unconscious of its approaching enemy. A column of vapor rose from the blowholes, like the escape of steam from a valve, twelve or fifteen feet into the air. We saw the harpooneer poised and erect, with his thigh braced in the clumsy cleat, his arms balancing the harpoon in readiness.

"Steady!" we heard him call. "Coming to wind'ard, sir! Starboard yer hellum, ye're gittin' on his eye!"

I remembered Messina Clarke telling me that a sperm whale's eyes are so placed that it commands a wide, oblique vision, thus rendering it able to guard against attack from either side. But the vulnerability of the monster lies in the fact that it cannot see an object that is directly fore and aft. Consequently "gittin' on his eye" meant entering the whale's line of vision.

The stillness of the scene was disturbed only by the chuckling of the restless ripples as they swashed against the sides of the *Catawba* and the gurgling of the rip tides as they played about her forefoot. We were taut with suspense. Now we could see the whale more plainly, see the bunch of the neck and the hump as they rose on the long swells, while the enormous flukes churned the water to a foam.

One of the crew of the whaler gave me his spyglass, for which I was deeply grateful. "Here, lad," he offered, "this ain't nothin' new to me. Cast yer eye along this glass, now, and see what you kin see."

Many times magnified within the circle of the glass, I could see water foaming over the dark head of the whale, exposing now and again the long, cruel jaw. The junk was scarred and seamed, testimony to many a fierce battle for supremacy with its own species, or perhaps with the giant octopus, its natural food and enemy. The mate of the whaleboat was laying a course head-on to the whale.

"Now, b'y!" we heard him call, "up and at him! Don't miss yer chance!"

But already the harpooneer had driven his blow. The weapon was buried to the hilt just aft the black fin. The water was lashed to sudden fury by a sweep of the flukes.

"Stern all!" yelled the mate, and the boat was instantly oared backward to clear the whale. "Are you fast, b'y?"

"Got one iron in, sir. Don't know about t'other."

The line leaped from the tub and went spinning around the loggerhead, through the chocks, a puff of smoke issuing forth from the friction. The whale had sounded and there was naught to do but wait for the rising.

Twenty minutes passed, but still the line was slowly running out of the tub, or taut. Another quarter of an hour . . . interminable it seemed to us watching, breathless, from the deck of the whaleship. Through my glass I could see the mate peering over the gunwhale; then his voice shouted:

"He's a-comin'! Haul line!"

Frantically now the men were hauling in the line and coiling it loosely on the platform.

"Coil that line clear, lads!" the mate barked. "Look out! Stern all! Here he comes!"

But the warning was too late. The whale, out of breath, rose with a blow and a puff. Water rushed off his back like the decks of a frigate clearing itself for action. The bunch of the monster's neck caught the keel of the boat and lifted it full out of water. It slewed off to larboard, spilling the men out on the whale's back, whence they slid off into the sea. The whale, enraged by all this business, swept his flukes, and in the sweep caught the heavy whaleboat and flung it high into the air as easily as a child might toss a ball. As it descended, a mighty sideswipe from the caudal smashed it to smithereens and left the splinters bobbing on the waves with the heads of the crew, who fully expected at any moment to meet their end in the whale's jaws. But the whale had had enough. With loops of line hanging in festoons from his teeth, he started off toward the horizon in a wake of boiling foam.

The Captain ordered a boat out to pick up the crew, who were treading water and supporting themselves by oars and bits of splintered planking. The mate was counting heads and soon all were present and accounted for. By this time the breeze had freshened and Captain Creesy gave the order to return to the *Flying Cloud*, after delivering several letters and messages to the commander of the *Catawba*.

That night in the foc'sle of the *Cloud* conversation revolved about naught but whaling. Even the prospect of approaching land was, for the moment, shouldered aside. Tom Plunkett snorted at the exhibition of whaling skill we had witnessed that day, and regaled us with tales of the days when whale fishing *was* something. Many hair-raising experiences he claimed to have had.

The breeze had freshened, and Captain Creesy gave the order to return to the *Flying Clou* of approaching land was, f

nat night in the foc'sle conversation revolved about naught but whaling. Even the prospect
e moment, shouldered aside.

"All on a sudden," he mused, "like a bolt o' lightnin' the jaws o' that whale—wi' two rows o' shiny teeth—shot out o' water. Next, the whole ruddy whale hisself lept clear into the air, carryin' wi' him the stem o' the boat. And there was Zeb Pound, hangin' from one corner o' the whale's mouth like a blinkin' sardine! Aye—sometimes now of nights I wake up seein' that pore sailor's face!"

Not to be outdone, Caleb Winthrop contributed his bit: "hamstringing" a whale with a boat spade.

"It takes a proper man to fight under the flukes of a whale," he declared with becoming modesty, while his eyes sparkled with recollection of youthful daring. "As you lads know, a whale ain't rigged like an ordinary fish with his flukes set fore and aft. Nope! They's set athwartships, jest like on a porpoise or a dolphin. When they wants to take a header, they've got to get a purchase with the flat o' their caudal, then throw it high up in the air to make their dive. Then's yer chance! You stands up in the bows and you swings yer spade with all yer might, right into the tendons that connect up the flukes wi' the body. That's the windup o' Mister Whale. Like a ship without a rudder he is, and proper hamstrung."

Small wonder, I thought, that tales of "spading flukes" live on in the memory of the old whalers and are rendered, even today, the homage that goes with a stout heart and nerves of iron.

*   *   *   *   *   *   *   *

The *Flying Cloud* was laying knots behind her on the last lap of her voyage. From 50° South, Atlantic, she had made the phenomenal run of seven days to 50° South, Pacific.

From that point, sweeping along in the heel of the trades, she crossed the Equator again in 17 days. We were now 71 days out of New York and with promise of a passage that would set a record for all time.

Excitement aboard ship ran high and speculation was furious. The men, with nine tenths of their wages mortgaged to the slop chest for clothes and tobacco, were betting the meager balance on her run. And every man aboard—save the mutineers who had been clapped back in the 'tweendecks, and the first mate, still padlocked in his cabin—was bending his utmost of strength to speed the *Cloud* to her goal. There was no labor too great, no ordeal too long. As day by day brought us nearer to the California coast, we railed against each slackening breeze that threatened to retard us, and blessed every sudden-rising squall that sped us on.

All the standing rigging was tarred down, decks sanded and holystoned. Spars and yards were scraped and varnished till they glistened like a shark's belly. Every scrap of bright-work came in for its polishing; the paint locker was opened up for fresh supplies and new halyards were rove. The *Flying Cloud* blossomed under all this attention, like a fine flower preening in the sun.

Nothing short of the most unseasonable calms, or unfore-seen disaster, could hold her back now. I swelled with an overwhelming pride in this, my ship; the ship I had watched from her very beginnings, had had an infinitesimal part in shaping and in sailing. I was filled with admiration for her record of doubling the Horn in the teeth of an all but disastrous storm. I wanted to shout aloud my joy in having had a part, however small, in this grand undertaking.

No premonition did I have of the disaster about to overtake us.

I had been sent below to the rope locker to fetch up a length of hemp. It was dark down there in the bowels of the ship, and silent save for ship sounds and the chuckling and lapping of the water against the outer hull. There was only the thickness of a few planks between me and the sea. I laid my hand against the wood and I could feel the sea outside, like the beat of a pulse. And I knew again that feeling which seldom left me: the *aliveness* of this ship of mine.

Moisture stood out in beads on curving bulkhead and dripped from trunneled stanchion. Down here the creakings and groanings of the ship came closer and were more real.

". . . As if you're trying to talk to me, *Flying Cloud.* What is it you want to say, old friend? That one of these bright days we'll raise land on your starboard bow? That you've made a record that will stand on history's pages as long as men's hearts quicken to fine adventure? I know that. No—it's something else you're saying. There's no joy in those creaks of yours. Sort of—ominous, somehow . . ."

What light there was filtered down from above through scattered cracks and crannies. Plague me, thought I, as I felt along the bulkhead for the door, why hadn't I brought a lantern? Anyway, there would be a lamp in its gimbal in the rope locker; that I knew. The door swung suddenly to my touch, and leaving it thus open, I entered the locker. The lamp gimbals—where were they? My match sputtered and flickered in the close air. A sudden draught. The door banged shut behind me. Out went the match.

"Blast it!" I muttered, fishing in vain through my pockets. "The last one, of course!"

A low chuckle reached my ear.

"Who's there!" I cried sharply.

Again the chuckle, while a voice said, "There'll be all the light you want in a minute, Thacher!"

"Sneed!" I felt my blood draining.

"Right you are, me bucko; Jeeter Sneed himself." The man laughed aloud now, mad laughter, horrible to hear. "Thought I was chained up like a rat to a bulkhead, didn't you? I could lie here and rot, eh?"

There was light in the rope locker now. It took a second for the significance of that to penetrate. *Light!* A glow that touched the arching stanchions, stabbed by sudden-leaping flame. In that flash the scene engraved itself on my retina: Jeeter Sneed, wasted to skeleton bone; broken irons dangling from his arms; life only in his eyes and in the grope of his fingers.

"I could die down here like a bloody foc'sle rat, eh?" he screamed. "I've sawed through tougher irons'n these!"

I backed toward the door. Fumbled for the latch. Another burst of flame, leaping. . . . Sneed was edging toward me.

"I swore I'd square accounts with you, Thacher. Git away from that door!"

"Keep back, Sneed! I've whipped you before and I can——"

The man was upon me. With a crash we struck the floor. Over and over we rolled. Chains clanking—bodies twisting—cries tearing our throats. Weak though Sneed was,

there was death in the clutch of his fingers as they fought for a grip on my throat.

The flames were mounting now. The heat was blasting.

". . . You're afire, *Flying Cloud!* You're . . ."

A blow from the irons, full in my face, hurled me backward into the flames. A scream tore the air: man in mortal anguish. Could that voice be mine? Hair burning—flesh. A wave of nausea swept me as a thousand knives stabbed at my body.

". . . You're afire, *Flying Cloud!* . . ."

I pulled myself to my knees. Somewhere a man was laughing, gibbering like an idiot. Shadows leaped like marionettes. I tore the flaming shreds of shirt from my flesh. Smoke was blinding me. . . . I—must see. Fire lighted the rope locker to sudden brilliance. A skeleton gibbering . . . twin points of light in its eyesockets . . . a point of light on its chin. . . . Ha, Sneed! Now I'll——

My muscles did it of themselves. A point of light on the chin. Every ounce of beef behind that blow. Bone against bone. Knuckles cracking up. Sneed—groaning on the floor. Silence.

A fathom of hemp fitted itself to my fist.

". . . Fire can't touch you, *Flying Cloud!* Not while I——"

My arms swung the rope with all the strength they could muster, beating back the flames. The smoke was so thick now. So thick. Couldn't see. Hard to—breathe. I——

". . . Hello, Messina Clarke! What're you doing here? One hand for the ship and one for myself, eh? Gor', that December wind has a bite to it! I can see the top of your

head, Donald McKay, bent over your table—that drafting
room of yours.   And you, *Flying Cloud!*   For you—for you
my youth.   My strength.   My life—if need be . . ."

*   *   *   *   *   *   *   *

I must have been waking from a sleep.   Waking, then
dozing off again.   Voices reached me from a great distance.
The mate's, saying: "All snug below, sir.   The lad, is he—
dead?"   The Old Man's voice answering, "Orter be,
but——"

I was in the dining saloon; I could see that.   On the
table.   Funny place to be.   What was that?   My arms?
Couldn't be.   I moved them.   No—wouldn't try that again.

There came a rush of feet overhead.   A wild shout
ringing clear.

"Land Ho-o-!   Land Ho-o-o-!"

California.   It's California, *Flying Cloud!*

What are you crying for, you fool!

CHAPTER X

Land Ho! A Nugget of Gold—A Ship Clears for China

ON THE afternoon of August 31, 1851, the *Flying Cloud* entered the Golden Gate, 89 days and 21 hours from New York. The fastest passage that had ever been made on that course. The hills surrounding the bay were wrapped in the arid warmth of dry midsummer. Until Telegraph Hill was rounded, no evidence of human habitation or civilization could be seen; only the crumbling earthworks at Fort Point and the dilapidated adobe of the *Presidio*, the old Mexican military post. Alcatraz Island was bare and white with the guano of countless sea birds that nested upon it and hatched their young. Wild oats, fresh and green to a sailor's eye, grew rank on the hills of Contra Costa, while herds of cattle grazed in the plains at their feet.

Once around Telegraph Hill, however, the scene sprang to life. As the harbor of San Francisco opened up before the *Flying Cloud*, a hundred ships of every rig and description could be seen lying at anchor. Clearly a magnet was drawing the commerce of the world to this spot—gold.

The *Cloud* skirted cautiously along the cove and around into the very center of the town. A town more bristling with excitement could not be imagined! Tents and rude dwellings dotted the hillsides. The gambling fraternity held possession of the field. The Mexican game of *monte* kept the gold forever on the move. Mercantile establishments were thronged with men of every age and condition, outfitting for the diggings. If the gold fever had been wracking the New England states, here it raged with all-consuming fury. The heart of the multitude was in the mines.

A thousand ships were said to have taken the Cape Horn route since the great news of '49. Old vessels, for the most part, long held to be unseaworthy and patched together to meet the exigencies of the hour. More than one of them had entered the Golden Gate with pumps working day and night. Instead of coming to anchor, they were run directly upon the flats of Mission Bay, there to end their sea-going days as hotels, boarding houses, gambling dens, and whatnot. The *Niantic*, a full-rigged ship that had bucked the winds of every sea, was floated up to what is now the very heart of San Francisco and there turned into a boarding house of sorts. A public entrance was hewn in her stout oak side and over the opening a sign announced:

Rest for the Weary and Storage for Trunks

The ship *Apollo* knew a similar fate, being converted into a saloon and gambling den. Across the way, the brig *Euphemia* had been purchased by the City Council for a prison, and here the mutineers of the *Flying Cloud*, with Mister Jones her erstwhile first mate, were taken pending trial.

I set down these things for you here, Reader, because it seems that the proper sequence of my tale so demands. Actually, however, it was many weeks after the *Cloud* had

come to anchor in San Francisco Bay before I learned them myself. On that fateful afternoon I lay on the line that divides consciousness from oblivion; now shifting to wind'ard, now to le'ward. A burning fog seemed to envelop me, a fever that wracked my body internally and tortured it without.

Sometimes a familiar face would pierce the fog: Whit's or Mister Andrews'; or perhaps a voice. I remember the strangeness of the ship coming to anchor; the rattle of her chains; the stillness that settled in her bones. I remember distant music, wild cheers, the thud of feet on deck, people around me. A voice, the Old Man's, saying, "Think he'll pull through, Doc?" Another voice, a strange one, replying: "Hm-m-m! If we can get him to the hospital, maybe." Hands, gentle as a woman's, lifted the bandages. . . . Nature knew a way: pain too great to bear became its own anesthetic, and the fog closed in again.

It lifted shortly for a while. A gentle motion rocked me. I was in a street. Faces, unfamiliar ones now, all around me . . . voices. . . . "Aye, burned to a blister . . . *Flying Cloud*, a'most done for, she was . . ." I saw the back of a head that I recognized: it was Lanny's. The poles of my stretcher were over his shoulders. Behind me a voice cried, "Ease up a little, Lanny!" That was Whit's voice.

When sustained consciousness first returned, I know not. I seemed to have come back from a long voyage and I was tired. I lay in a lengthy room of frame construction, high on the slopes of a hill. There was no glass in the big window openings, only a sort of netting to keep out the flies and mosquitoes. A fresh breeze swept through the room, blowing the white sheets of the sick beds and stirring the hair on

One of the men—a landsman by the cut of his jib—I had never seen before.
The other was Captain Josiah Perkins Creesy.   The Old Man.

many a hot forehead. The only nurses were two Sisters of Mercy, moving silently through the ward in their dark robes. Something in each of those pure noble faces, sheltered within its starched headdress, reminded me of my mother, and brought a sudden pang of homesickness sharper even than the pains that knifed my body.

I had found that it was wiser to lie still than to move; to take shallow breaths instead of deep ones. I knew that my head was wrapped in sticky bandages leaving only my eyes and nose exposed. My arms and hands were bound about as well, but what my body might be like under the enveloping covers I did not know. Out of the clew of my eye I could see a sick man in the beds on either side of me. Silent men they were; one with his eyes closed; the other staring off into space. Who were they? Who could say with what high hopes they had started out, or what despair gnawed at them now? Somewhere a man was crying out. . . . One of the sisters was comforting him, gently, as if he had been a little shaver. Soon he fell asleep.

"I cal'late you must o' burned your tongue as well as the rest o' you!" It was Lanny's voice. How long had he been sitting there?

"For half a watch you haven't said a ruddy word," he complained. "Eyes wide open, too."

"I—didn't know you were here," I answered. "Can't shift my head around much. Tell me—the news."

"Aye, news there is aplenty, me hearty!" he answered, his young voice alive with eagerness. "The whole town's gone daft over the *Flying Cloud!* Ther's placards pasted on every bollard; 89 days and 21 hours from New York, anchor to anchor. Think of it, Thach! Nobody ever heard the like of it before. Mister Andrews says we've made history. The *Cloud's* freight rates are rocketing. They're unloading her in two shakes of a clew line to clear for China. Another record she'll set there, or I can't see a hole through a ladder!"

"How about—Sneed?"

"Dead as a herring, he is. Aye, suffocated and burned to death when they found him."

"And the mate?"

"Ho! *Mister* Jones?" he chortled. "He's locked up in the brig *Euphemia*, with the rest o' them packet rats. Tighter'n weevils in hardtack. I'd hate to stand in their sea boots. Mutiny on the high seas, they're charged with. Aye, it won't go easy with them! These-here 'Frisco folks are what they calls Vigilantys and they don't hold with law-breakers of any sort."

"And the Old Man?"

Lanny's face beamed. "They're dinin' and winin' him like he was a king or somethin'. The Owners gave him a big dinner at the Parker House last night and a silver service to take back to his lady."

"When is the *Cloud* clearing for—China?" It was hard to bring out those words. I knew the answer.

"Most any day now, Thach."

Against my will my eyes looked down at my hands in their many wrappings. Lanny's eyes followed mine.

"Gor', Thach!" he cried, his voice straining. "You'll be all right in a day or two and ready to fist a r'yal as well as ever!" His friendly face was bending over me. Something splashed on my nose.

One of the sisters laid a hand on Lanny's arm. "I'm afraid you'll have to go now," she said softly, "but you can come back again tomorrow if you like."

My eyes followed Lanny as he moved down the ward. There was the swing of the sea in his walk and in the lift of his head; and I sought the open window with its far view of the Pacific, blue and ruffling in the afternoon wind. Ships out there in the harbor looked like toy boats with handkerchiefs spread for sails. The ladder of the sunbeams slanted out the window and upward, like the shrouds of some heroic vessel whose main-truck was a star. All very well to dream dreams, thought I mournfully, but dreams have to be paid for in one coin or another. Dreams of spice islands lying in another sea; of black-sailed frigates whose decks ran dark with pirate blood; of the miracle of the albatross wheeling through wastes of lonely sky; of the sperm whale heaving his varnished hulk to the surface to throw a jet of rainbow mist high into the air—all very well those dreams, as long as you kept them at home where they belonged. But I had shipped with mine to sea.

The door at the far end of the ward opened. A sister in her black robe entered, followed by two men. One of the men—a landsman by the cut of his jib—I had never seen before. The other was Captain Josiah Perkins Creesy. The Old Man.

"Well, Thacher, me b'y, how are you?" The Old Man's voice boomed through the room. Though he tried to mute it in consideration of the sick, forty years of skys'l shouting echoed in his thunders.

"I'm fine, sir."

There was a ship out there beating across the bay with all canvas spread.
Clean-lined and eager as a greyhound she was; the core and essence of a
ship; all pride and beauty and strength.

"This is Mr. Webster, the western representative of Grinnell's." A wave of his hand included the stranger.

The man smiled. "Glad to know ye, lad."

"Well, Thacher," said Captain Creesy, clearing his throat, "the doctor tells me it'll be another month before you'll be up and about. And some time longer before you'll be able to use those hands again."

"Yes, sir. I—know. The *Cloud* will be in China by then."

The Old Man laid his hand on my shoulder. "There's no place on a ship for a sick man, lad," he said kindly. "I've arranged with the captain of the *Sargasso* to ship you home with him next month. I misdoubt you'll be able to work your passage, but you can thank Mr. Webster, here, for extending this courtesy on behalf of Grinnell's."

"Thank you, sir."

"And one other thing, Thacher." The Old Man cleared his throat again, and seemed suddenly ill at ease. "We—the Company, that is, has—has got something here for you!"

One of his hands fumbled in the pocket of his blue-serge coat and produced a small box tied about with string. His fingers picked clumsily at the knots.

"Shall I do it?" asked the sister, smiling. Her hands were deft with small things, and in no time the box was open. An exclamation escaped her. "Ah, how beautiful it is! See!"

In the palm of her hand lay a nugget from the gold fields. It shone with a warm, friendly glow. One side of it was slightly flattened out and polished.

Captain Creesy chuckled. "Read what's engraved on it, Thacher," he said.

"I—I can't, sir."

"I'll read it for you," offered the sister. "It says: 'Enoch Thacher. Ship *Flying Cloud* 1851. For a great service bravely performed.'"

*   *   *   *   *   *   *   *

The morning dawned bright with gold, as all these mornings seemed to do. In the ward, men had not yet begun to stir. I could hear the steady rhythm of their breathing. By the door one of the sisters sat asleep in her chair, her face hidden under the droop of her white headdress.

The wind blew through the open window, tonic with life. The waters of the Golden Gate fretted within the circling hills. I lifted my head a trifle, the better to see. A southeasterly breeze was blowing across the bay, whipping the water into cresting wavelets. Cloud shadows darkened the surface as they passed. There was a ship out there, beating across the bay with all canvas spread. Clean-lined and eager as a greyhound; the core and essence of a ship: all pride and beauty and strength. From her stem sprang the figure of an angel with trumpet poised, like a herald of good tidings, and almost it seemed I could hear the wild gladness of the trumpet blast. Out through the Golden Gate—China bound.

As she passed into the reaches of the wide Pacific, she dipped her ensign. Only a routine courtesy of a ship leaving port; not a signal, I knew. Yet, perhaps——

"Did you want something?" a gentle voice asked.

"No, Sister."

"I thought I heard you call!"

THE END

NAUTICAL GLOSSARY

A FIRST AID FOR THE LANDLUBBER

⊗

Backstays, wire ropes which are abaft the shrouds, supporting the strain on the masts.

Belaying pin, wooden or iron bars to which running gear is made fast, or "belayed."

"Belaying-pin soup," Jack's expression for the rough-and-tumble tactics of a bucko mate.

Binnacle, a stand or box containing a ship's compass and a light for use at night.

Bollard, an upright post of wood or iron, around which to take a turn with a rope.

Bollard timber (see knighthead).

Bonito, a fish somewhat like a large, solid mackerel, with a firm flesh that is very tasty to a sea-going palate.

Bosun bird, a sea bird with cream-colored plumage, long tail feathers, and a beak somewhat like that of a snipe.

Braced up, when the yards of a square-rigger are on the backstays to a wind before the beam, a ship is said to be "braced up."

Brail, a rope fastened to the leech or corner of a sail and leading through a block, by which the sail can be hauled up or in, preparatory to furling.

Bunt, the middle part of a square sail; or the part of a furled sail that is gathered up in a roll at the center of the yard.

Cathead, an out-jutting baulk of timber, used to suspend an anchor over the bows.

Catting, when an anchor has been made fast to the cathead, it is said to be "catted."

Clew, to haul a sail by means of clew garnets, clew lines, etc., up to a yard or mast.

Clew jigger, a small tackle used instead of clew lines to trice up the clew of a sail.

Clew line, a rope by which a clew of an upper square sail is hauled up to its yard.

Clew rope, a rope for hauling up the clews of spankers or trysails.

Close-hauled, when a square-rigger is sailing on a wind with her yards braced sharp-up on the backstays, she is "close-hauled."

Colza oil, a vegetable oil used in binnacle lights.

Corposant, or "St. Elmo's Fire"; an electrical phenomenon seen on a ship during a storm; held in superstitious awe by the old shellback.

Courses, the foresail, mainsail, and cro'jik.

Devilfish, a fish like an aquatic bat, with wings and a barbed tail, its mouth placed well underneath its head.

173

Dogwatches, the two watches of two hours each, between four and eight P.M.

Dolphin, a fish of numerous species; the bottle-nosed dolphin commonly called *porpoise.*

Doldrums, the latitudes of "calms and variables," lying between the northeast and southeast trade winds, in both the Atlantic and Pacific oceans.

Fiferail, a heavy rail of wood, on each side of the masts where running gear is made fast to belaying pins.

"Fishing," a fish-shaped piece of timber used to strengthen a mast or yard.

Figurehead, a carved and painted ornament that decorates the apex of a ship's stem.

Flying fish, an inhabitant of tropic waters, somewhat like a herring, with gauzy wings that enable it to achieve a skimming "flight" over the surface of the sea.

Flying-fish weather, Jack's expression for the halcyon days in the latitudes inhabited by the flying fish.

Frigate bird, or "man-o'-war"; a sea bird with wings of immense power; it does not swim and so must snatch its fish from the other birds.

Full and by, when a square-rigger is being steered on a wind with her canvas full, she is sailing "full and by."

"Gamming," a term used by whalemen, referring to the visits between the crews of ships at sea.

Gammoning band, a metal band or chain lashing, securing the bowsprit to the stemhead.

Grampus, a cetacean allied to the blackfish, but having teeth in the lower jaw only.

Handspike, a round length of wood with a squared end, used to heave lashings tight and setting up lanyard rigging.

Harness cask, a large teakwood receptacle in which Jack's "salt horse" is kept soaking in brine.

Haze, a word that meant much to a sailor in the '50's; if an officer threatened "hazing," it meant punishment by work of the most grueling sort.

Holystone, a rough stone the size of a large Bible, for scouring the decks; an invention of the Devil despite the sanctimony of its name.

"Humbugged," when a sailor felt that he had been kept at a needless task, he was being put upon, or "humbugged."

"Irishman's hurricane," Jack's expression for a driving vertical rain.

Keelhauling, ridding a ship's keel of barnacles by means of a grating hauled back and forth; also a method of hazing a sailor.

Knighthead, a timber rising just within the stem in a ship, on either side of the bowsprit.

Lazaret, the space aft, below the cabin quarters, for storing provisions.

Leech, either edge of a square sail.

Leeward, the direction toward which the wind is blowing; pronounced "looard."

Magellan Clouds, three small nebulæ in the southern skies; first seen just above the horizon after crossing the southern tropic.

Marlinespike, a metal spike with a sharp point, used to open the strands when splicing wire rope.

Monkey rail, a low railing running around the poop.

Packet rat, a term of contempt used by sailors of the windships toward the men who manned the packets.

Poop, the elevated structure of the deck aft, beneath which the officers have their quarters.

Pooped, a running ship overtaken by a following sea.

Portuguese man-o'-war, the Nautilus of the southern seas; these little fish have delicate "sails" of iridescent color.

Pound-and-pint, the meager rations allowed to the foremast hand.

Ratlines, small lines fastened across a ship's shrouds, like the rungs of a ladder.

Reef-earing, a length of heavy point line, for use in reefing a sail.

Relieving tackle, used in dirty weather; a tackle hooked onto the tiller beneath the wheelbox, to prevent the wheel from "kicking" in a heavy sea.

Ring rope, a chain used in "catting" an anchor.

Sea lawyer, a term of approbrium, which has its synonym in "land shark."

Sennit, rope yarns worked up into rovings, to lash the heads of the sails to the jackstay.

Shrouds, a set of ropes forming part of the standing rigging, and supporting mast or topmast.

Slop Chest, a deep-sea institution which takes recognition of Jack's improvidence by having on board ship a supply of boots, oilskins, tobacco, etc., which can be purchased and charged against his wages.

"Sogering," loafing on the job.

Soul-and-body lashings, rope yarns passed around a sailor's oilskins at waist, ankles, and wrists.

Southern Cross, four bright stars in the form of a rude cross; begins to be seen at 18° N., and in the vicinity of Cape Horn is nearly overhead.

Splicing the main brace, Jack's expression for imbibing strong liquor.

Spun yarn, marline, seizing stuff, etc., are made on board out of old ropes which the sailors unlay; then drawing out the yarns, they knot them together and roll them up in balls.

Tarring down, swung aloft in a bosun's chair, with pot of tar and a bunch of oakum, Jack "tars down" the standing rigging.

Trick, a spell, or "trick" of two hours at the wheel.

Windlass, any of various mechanical devices for hauling or hoisting.

Windward, the direction from which the wind is blowing; pronounced "wind'ard."